Dedalus Europe 2014
General Editor: Mike Mitchell

# God's Dog

*Diego Marani*

# God's
# Dog

Translated by Judith Landry

Dedalus

This book has been published with the support of Ministero Affari Esteri Italiano and Arts Council England, London.

Supported using public funding by
**ARTS COUNCIL
ENGLAND**

Published in the UK by Dedalus Limited,
24-26, St Judith's Lane, Sawtry, Cambs, PE28 5XE
email: info@dedalusbooks.com
www.dedalusbooks.com

ISBN printed book  978 1 909232 51 8
ISBN ebook  978 1 909232 87 7

Dedalus is distributed in the USA & Canada by SCB Distributors,
15608 South New Century Drive, Gardena, CA 90248
email: info@scbdistributors.com   web: www.scbdistributors.com

Dedalus is distributed in Australia by Peribo Pty Ltd.
58, Beaumont Road, Mount Kuring-gai, N.S.W. 2080
email: info@peribo.com.au

*Publishing History*
First published in Italy in 2012
First published by Dedalus in 2014

*Il Cane di Dio* © copyright Diego Marani 2012
Published by arrangement with Marco Vigevani Agenzia Letteraria

The right of Diego Marani to be identified as the author & Judith Landry as the translator of this work has been asserted by them in accordance with the Copyright, Designs and Patents Act, 1988.

Printed in Finland by Bookwell
Typeset by Marie Lane

# Diego Marani

Diego Marani was born in Ferrara in 1959. He is a policy officer of the European Commission in charge of the European multilingualism policy. He is the inventor of the mock-European language Europanto in which he has been writing columns for newspapers and magazines all over Europe for many years. His collection of short stories in Europanto, *Las Adventures des Inspector Cabillot*, has been published by Dedalus.

He is the author of six novels including the highly acclaimed *New Finnish Grammar* and *The Last of the Vostyachs*.

Dedalus will publish his third novel *The Interpreter* in 2015.

# Judith Landry

Judith Landry was educated at Somerville College, Oxford where she obtained a first class honours degree in French and Italian. She combines a career as a translator of works of fiction, art and architecture with part-time teaching.

Her translations for Dedalus are: *New Finnish Grammar* and *The Last of the Vostyachs* by Diego Marani, *The House by the Medlar Tree* by Giovanni Verga, *The Devil in Love* by Jacques Cazotte, *Prague Noir: The Weeping Woman on the Streets of Prague* by Sylvie Germain and *Smarra & Trilby* by Charles Nodier.

# Disclaimer

# I

'*My name is Domingo Salazar, I was born on the feast of Saint Dominic and brought up by the Dominican Fathers. I am a policeman, I see to it that the laws of our Holy Mother Church are respected and I work for the worldwide spread of that same Church. I never knew my parents, but from the colour of my skin I think they must have been Caribbean, or at least of mixed race. The fathers found me beneath the rubble of the orphanage of the Holy Cross, in Haiti, in 2010, and brought me to Italy. I grew up in the boarding-school run by the Dominican sisters of Saint Imelda, I studied at the patriarchal monastery in Bologna and then at the Papal Police Academy in Rome, which I left with the rank of inspector in the fifth year of the reign of Pope Benedict XVIII.*'

He had developed this mania for diary-keeping as a result of the time he had spent with the nuns. 'Time to get writing!' the mother superior would say after tea, throwing open the grey door to the wood-panelled main hall. You still wrote with pen and paper in those days, in an exercise-book backed with black cloth which was chained to the desk, and which the sisters would read through later. So this diary had become a detailed account of his life, divided up into years. But Domingo Salazar

7

would always copy out those first same sentences in every new exercise-book he began, as though to remind himself of who he was.

It was almost time for his appointment. Outside it was already dark. He had slept much of the afternoon; he had thrown himself on to the bed the moment he'd arrived, without even opening his suitcase. His flight had left at dawn, and he'd spent the whole previous night writing, as he always did. He washed himself in cold water, then shaved and dressed slowly in front of the mirror in the bathroom. He picked up his pistol holster from the chair and strapped it on under his arm. He didn't like the sound of this new mission. He didn't yet know much about it, but hunting down angels of death was a job for an ordinary municipal policeman, not an inspector like himself. Those Free Death Brigades struck him as amateurs, hot-heads with few means and even less experience. For all he knew, they might not even be organized into a proper group; they were stray dogs embarking on wild-goose chases. But orders were orders, and at seven o'clock he would learn further details about his assignment from the vicar.

He arrived at Sant'Andrea della Valle just as evening mass was ending. The priest gave the blessing and the faithful started trooping out. Salazar went up to the confessional to the right of the nave. The curtain was half-open, but the priest's seat was empty, as was the one in the other confessional to the left. He walked up and down, pretending to examine the frescoes, then went back into the apse. By now the church was empty, except for an altar-boy who was putting out the candles. Salazar decided to go and kneel before one of the two confessionals at random, imagining that the vicar, were he in the church, would come and join him. An agent and his vicar must never see or know each other; they were not to use mobiles or email; communication between them had to be exclusively oral. This was the number one safety rule for the secret agents of the papal police. The meeting-place was a confessional in the church referred to in the mission order, itself the only written document – unsigned – which would remain in the registers of the barracks to which the agent in question belonged. When an agent on a mission lost contact with his vicar, he had to present himself at the nearest Swiss Guards post for an identity check. That was the only way he could be reinstated in the corps. Otherwise he himself became an outlaw, and might be eliminated. Salazar went back into the nave and up to the nearest confessional, the one on the left. Coming from the chapel, he couldn't see the seat but, as he approached, he saw two black shoes on the footstool. Well, he thought, the vicar's here at last. He was about to kneel down when the purple curtain was nudged aside by an elbow; for one brief instant, Salazar saw the fingertips of two white hands holding a glass bulb, witnessed the delicate gesture made by a one-eyed man slipping his prosthesis into an empty socket. Then the curtain was almost closed again, and the man's face was sunk in shadow. Embarrassed by his unintentional intrusion, Salazar took a few steps backwards before going to kneel down, hoping that the vicar had not noticed anything. He could hear breathing through the openwork grille. As agreed, he recited the Credo, gave his registration number and then waited, in silence.

'Inspector Salazar, I know you to be a faithful soldier in the service of our Holy Mother Church. I know your superiors, and they have confirmed your gifts in this regard. Furthermore

I know you to have an excellent record, a decoration and various recommendations. I also know about your activities in Beirut and I congratulate you on them. We could do with more agents with such initiative! If I have called you here from Amsterdam, it is because I have a delicate task to entrust to you. You see, of all the dangers threatening our Holy Mother Church, none is more terrible than the practice of free death, which is becoming ever more widespread in this depraved world of ours. Euthanasia, as miscreants and scientists refer to it, destroys what God holds dearest, namely, the life He has given us. Euthanasia does away with the mystery of pain, which should be so revered. It's not just a question of dogma, Salazar. Our hold on people's consciences is also at stake. If men cease to fear death, or begin to regard it as something run-of-the-mill, our sway over them is seriously threatened. We are already conducting an active campaign of propaganda and dissuasion, but it's no longer enough. What is called for is repression, carefully handled, and above all covert. People must not be aware of the restraints which bind them. The first part of your mission will be this, Salazar. You will inspect the hospitals in the fourth zone and keep an eye on such terminally-ill patients as might be seeking death. You will need to know everything about them, every last detail of their lives. You will have to glean information about their relatives, their friends, their intimate ties. You will have to delve into their past and know their every ambition and achievement. And also what they own: because, as you well know, inspector, the law authorizes the Church to seize the goods of those who die an unnatural death, and this is a powerful weapon in our armoury. Even the most ardent euthanasiast thinks twice before seeing his own children disinherited. You will also keep a close eye on the medical staff. As we know, despite the purges, many abortionists are still active within their ranks. Even the smallest detail should be taken into account, Salazar. You will have to keep the closest watch on every dying man. You will have to be able to tell from their expressions if theirs is willing suffering, or if they are rebelling against their fate. That is when they fall under the spell of the fanatics. We know that euthanasiasts make converts in hospitals. There they have a captive audience, and it is easy to convince sick people that they might wish to hasten their own end. But if you succeed in breaking this vicious circle, then we shall deprive them of their main sources of financial support. Because – and it is important to remember this – the sick actually pay to have themselves disposed of! It is only by thwarting their hold over sick people that we shall ultimately succeed in routing the angels of death!'

The vicar was gripping the handrail of the confessional with such force that it positively creaked. Even through the brass grating, Salazar felt the priest's breath on his face. It was that smell of musty material and mouthwash which were subsequently to inform him of the vicar's presence.

'Now for the second part of your mission, inspector, the more tricky part: a manhunt. For years we've been trying to track down Ivan Zago, an abortionist doctor who works underground. We know that he has fled abroad; he's currently living in Switzerland, where we are powerless to lay hands on him. We've had his parents under surveillance for some time, hoping to intercept him; they are the only members of his family who have stayed on in Italy. But some time ago we lost track of them. His mother is probably dead. We're not certain, but she seems to have been buried in a common grave in the

Flaminio Cemetery. We didn't know anything about his father, either, until various clues led us to the Hospital of San Filippo Neri, where it seems that a certain Davide Zago was admitted with a brain tumour three months ago, and then discharged, according to the hospital register. But the address on his hospital file is false, as is the name of the doctor who was caring for him. In a word, we suspect that Davide Zago is still in that hospital, probably dying, hidden among the terminal patients. His son Ivan will be ready to do anything to spare him a lingering death. He will try to reach him in hospital to help him die, with the help of the accomplices who had him hidden there. And that's where we must set our trap, inspector! The bait of the father will lead us to the son!'

'But if we don't know what name Zago is going under, how can we be certain that he's still in San Filippo Neri and not another hospital?'

'We can't. That's why we've installed agents in the other Roman hospitals. But everything points to San Filippo Neri. Davide Zago was recognized by two nurses at the time he was admitted, so we're sure that it was him. After the operation we lost track of him. Someone falsified his hospital files. But in the oncology ward there turns out to have been one patient more than there are beds. And in the last three months no terminally-ill patient has been transferred from San Filippo Neri.'

'I see. Does anyone at the hospital know of my mission?'

'Only the Medical Guarantor of Faith. He'll be expecting you. You are to introduce yourself to the department as an assistant pilgrim priest. Thousands of pilgrim priests are arriving in Rome for the canonization of Benedict XVI. No one will be surprised by your presence in the hospital.'

The vicar fell silent. Salazar heard a rustling of cloth from behind the grille and couldn't help thinking about the glass eye he'd just seen.

'One more thing, inspector. Leaflets issued by the Free Death Brigade have been found around the city. These people are dangerous terrorists who will stop at nothing. They are financed by foreign powers and other enemies of the Church. There is a risk that they may be preparing to strike on Easter Day, when Benedict XVI is to be canonized. The security services are on red alert. In the past we've discovered some of their hiding-places and seized various pieces of propaganda material. But this time something more serious is afoot. What we fear even more than the threat of a massacre itself is the spectacular nature of the possible attack. The whole world would be abuzz, and that is something we can never countenance. That is why the arrest of some abortionist or other enemy of the faith would serve our purpose. They might lead us to the Free Death Brigades. We must make them feel that we are on their heels! You may go now, inspector. Leave the church and do not linger. I'll be waiting for you here every Friday after evening mass, so call by if you have anything to report'. The priest fell silent and withdrew into the darkness. Salazar stayed there motionless for a few moments and smelt a slight whiff of scent coming from the other side of the grille; a pleasant smell of strawberries spread through the air.

Even without seeing his interlocutor, the inspector knew instinctively what kind of man the vicar was: one of the old guard, a man who had lived through troubled times and then witnessed the birth of the Catholic Republic. In a word, an old zealot who saw enemies of the faith at every turn. Number 2354 of the Catholic Catechism, as redrafted by His Holiness Benedict XVI in 2005, runs as follows: *The citizen is conscience-bound to ignore the orders of the civil authorities when these run counter to the demands of the moral order, to fundamental rights or the teachings of the Gospel.* It was this that led many Catholics to rebel against the godless laws of the Italian Republic. When parliament rejected the first proposal for a law which, in accordance with paragraph 2354, made offences against chastity a crime, together with homosexuality, masturbation and fornication, there were outbursts of protest all over Italy, and a state of emergency was declared. Salazar was still a pupil at the patriarchal monastery at the time, but he had clear memories of the atmosphere of frenzy and alarm which marked the months preceding the New Concordat.

That autumn, the prior began delivering solemn lectures which talked of invisible enemies. We listened without understanding and, as we came out of the refectory where the priest would have us gather to hear his sermons, we were too scared to discuss them. For some months, lessons were given in the cramped classrooms which overlooked the courtyard rather than in the airy rooms overlooking the street. The Saturday walk was now a thing of the past. Pupils were allowed out only when accompanied by a guardian, in small groups and always in civilian clothes. Canons and novices alike spent a gloomy winter staring out of the refectory window watching the snow piling up on the roofs and then melting away. That was their only glimpse of the outside world. But Salazar also remembered that Sunday the following spring when the pope paid a visit to Bologna. That had been a memorable day. The bells rang out as they had never rung before. The fathers had received the news of the visit with trepidation. As time went by, relief was visible on their faces, as though some impending danger had been averted. As the event approached, they looked increasingly self-confident, and positively triumphant when the papal procession arrived at San Petronio. The square was heaving with little white and yellow flags. Salazar was in the first row of novices, lined up on the flight of steps in their splendid uniforms. Of all their number, it was he upon whom the pope had chosen to bestow his blessing.

Since then, almost twenty years had gone by. The Catholic Republic was by now on a firm footing. Internal dissent was minimal. The anti-papists preferred to leave Italy rather than mount any opposition. The pope's rule was no longer in jeopardy. But a few hard-line canons still remained in the hierarchy. Such was their prestige that it was impossible to oust them from their posts. They still had the power to have people placed under surveillance, even bishops. Salazar sighed as he left the church. This was the kind of manhunt that would end in death. He would have preferred to have stayed in Amsterdam, busying himself with the Counter-Reformation, as he put it. That was something he did well. He was a hooligan at heart; he liked destroying things. He drew comfort from the fact that his mission in Rome would be short-lived. Wherever he was, with a brain tumour Davide Zago was not long for this world.

Salazar ate in a little restaurant in the Campo Marzio, then wandered through the narrow streets and, without realizing it, found himself back at the convent. It was still early, and he was not remotely tired. Nevertheless, he pushed open the main door, turned the key in the inner gate and went into the tiled entrance hall, which smelled of vinegar. A light was on in the corridor, but no noise came from beyond the glass doors. Those Carmelite Nuns had struck him as strange from the moment he arrived. There seemed too few of them for a convent of that size. The mother superior had told him that building work was going on, to turn the place into a proper pilgrims' hospice, but he had never seen any sign of activity on his wanderings through the corridors. All that was to be seen were crates of books and old furniture packed up for some imminent move. Even the little chapel on the ground floor seemed disused. The nuns attended mass in the Cantonese Church on the other side of the street. The candle in front of the statue of the Virgin in the niche on the main staircase flickered as he walked past.

He had not noticed how large his room was when he arrived that morning: there were ten good paces between bed and table. He threw open the shutters and breathed in the damp air. It had stopped raining, but the wind was getting up.

His room looked out on to a courtyard, with galleries and terraces. Puddles of water rippled beneath the pots of rhododendrons; water was dripping from the eaves. Beyond the roofs, the side of the church was visible in the lamplight. Every so often, the sound of traffic would drift in. Down in the narrow streets, he could hear the sound of voices, calling each other, laughing. Domingo Salazar unzipped the inner pocket of his suitcase and took out an object which looked like a holy-water sprinkler. He unscrewed the cap, took out a cigarette holder from the handle and put a small Dutch clay pipe into his mouth. He kept his Afghan black in a small enamelled box, together with his ear-plugs. He filled the brazier, lit the resin and allowed himself a mocking grin. Disguising his pipe as a holy-water sprinkler gave him a sense of deep satisfaction. It was a pity that no one ever had the temerity to search an agent of the papal police force. At the sight of his badge, even the Swiss Guards would back off. He felt the better for his smoke. He closed the window, put his black exercise-book on the table, opened it, lit the lamp and began to write.

*Every time I come back to Italy I am seized by a sense of puzzlement. Here they have not yet understood that, in the West, conversion is no longer the way to extend the Church's power. Western man is no longer susceptible to conversion; he is like those germs which become resistant to antibiotics. He cannot believe, even despite himself; he is too sure of what he knows. We persist in trying to bring the Church closer to the people. We ought to be doing the reverse: making it more remote, not more accessible. Restoring a sense of mystery. But not so that man may experience a facile, all-absolving sense of beatitude. No, man must feel impelled to revere God, to placate his wrath. Fear is of the essence. We should go back to the root of religion, which is above all fear of God. We should begin by reintroducing sacrifice. Did not the ancient Jews slaughter lambs on the altar? The sacrificial victim which draws evil to itself is always an excellent nostrum for the masses. Joseph Ratzinger said as much in his catechism: 'The Lord is to be worshipped with words of praise, and thanks, and supplication; and by the offering up of sacrifices.' We have silenced the organs in our cathedrals and replaced them with guitars. But, by so doing, we have dispelled the fear of the numinous, and churches have become places of entertainment. Here in Italy, where the Church holds sway, the police are hunting down euthanasiasts; as though, by apprehending the odd suicide, atheism might be kept at bay. This is the mistake of those who delude themselves that they can win back a society which is completely lacking any sense of the divine. The curia fails to understand that the only way to re-establish the power of the Church is through immigration. Let us allow ourselves to be drowned out by millions without any hope, and that is how we shall hold sway over them. The strategy of the tenth parallel no longer makes any sense. It is useless to persist in defending a frontier between Christianity and Islam. That is no longer the line to be held. What we should be doing is getting out of the trenches, start fighting in the open. In Africa, our worst enemies are not the Muslims, but the Pentecostalists. So the way forward in reconquering the West is to import fresh masses of dispossessed humanity, Christian or otherwise, even the Polynesians with their pig god Kamapua'a. All that matters is that they be believers. Kamapua'a or Christ, for us it is immaterial, so long as there is faith.*

While he was writing, a postcard had slipped out of the exercise-book; an old postcard, of the kind now found only on junk-stalls. Slightly faded, with wavy edges and a blue postmark. Salazar found himself peering at the little town of Veere, in Zeeland, at the little harbour, in whose still waters the imposing outline of the Grote Kerk was reflected. It looked like an overturned ship, covered with seaweed and shells. He lifted the postcard to his lips, reread the few words with a smile and slipped it back between the blank pages.

At that same moment, in a garage in Malagrotta, a man and a woman were getting out of a white van.

'From tomorrow onwards I'll be at Monte Spaccato. You'll have to deal with the explosives on your own,' said the woman, opening the van door.

'We and the others will see to that. We've already made arrangements with Mirko. On Tuesday we're seeing the Russians. We'll be making two trips. They want to give us the components in two instalments; for reasons of security, they say. They're cautious people, but that's no bad thing. Clearly, they know what they're doing. The service area just before Civitavecchia, as usual. We'll put everything together here in the basement. When will you have finished at San Filippo Neri?' the man asked. He had turned off the engine. The light from the dashboard lit up his bearded face.

'It depends on how things go. Usually I need three or four days. I'll be doing the next one too, at the Gemelli. Then we'll have to stop and lie low for a bit. Until things calm down.'

'So, if all goes well, for quite some time!' said the man with a nervous grin, locking the door of the van.

'If all goes well…' the woman murmured into the darkness.

Neither the black jacket, worn over a collarless grey shirt, nor the silver crucifix, sported in the buttonhole, could fool the sister on the palliative care ward. Despite his dress, she knew immediately that he was not one of those pilgrim priests who did good works for the Church in order to pay for their stay in Rome. But she proceeded as though she suspected nothing, checking the registration number he gave her on the computer. Then she nodded, and opened the door to the office. Dawn was just breaking. The neon lights in the corridors of San Filippo Neri were beginning to go out.

'Sister, how many patients have you got on this ward?'

'Twenty-seven. All stable. Nine unconscious.'

'Atheists?'

'Four. All open and above board. All paying the official atheism tax.'

'And the others?'

'Twenty Catholics. Three Muslims.'

'Do they receive visits from an imam?'

'Every Friday.'

'What time do you celebrate lauds for the Catholics?'

'At seven every morning.'

'Do their relatives attend regularly?'

'All except for three. But the chaplain is authorized to act as proxy; and they pay the fine.'

'Are their ecclesial documents up-to-date?'

'We check them every time they come. All relatives have attended the requisite number of masses. But there have been lapses in the past, and they have been noted down.'

'Thank you. Tomorrow I'll need a list of the names and addresses of all the patients and their civil status. I'll leave it here with you; but it must always be available.'

'Very good'.

'Are we still in time for lauds?'

'The chaplain is waiting for me. Come this way.'

Salazar followed the sister through the glazed door. Several empty camp beds stood in the corridor, over whose light brown linoleum a cleaning women was wearily pushing a mop. The smell of the detergent mingled with the scent of coffee and cut flowers; some rooms were full of them. As he entered the large room, Salazar was instantly struck by the winking of bubbles in innumerable drips, the only things in that whole space that moved at all. Heavy white globs, they rose to the surface, then sank down again, unceasing in their regularity. The beds were arranged in two rows in front of an improvised altar, rigged up on a piece of furniture originally from a chemist's shop. Several stretcher-bearers had just brought in the most recent arrivals, and were now quietly leaving. The relatives remained, like so many unmoving sentinels. Filtering in through the curtains, the daylight could not contend with the soft, tenacious shadow. Some patients were groaning, dark hands moving spasmodically over the dense white of the sheets. But the chaplain soon drowned the sound out with his prayers.

'Lord of all mercy, may your victims' prayers come unto you; show them the light which frees man from all pain! You are the life eternal, you are the way, the truth.'

'Show them the light!' chorused the shadowy figures in sepulchral unison. Salazar immediately sensed a jarring note, a lying note, among those voices. Lauds was a group prayer for which the patients in every ward in the hospital were brought together once a day. Visiting relatives were expected to join in. For the terminally ill it was an opportunity to take a reckoning, to see just how close their fellow-sufferers were to death. Only those who had received extreme unction were spared the lauds. But, for fear of reprisals, many relatives did not even dare ask for it. At the end of the rite the stretcher-bearers pushed the beds back into the rooms from which they had come, and suffering could carry on unimpeded.

The Medical Guarantor of Faith was a bony, shambling man with long, vein-threaded hands. He sported an eye-catching white goatee which he moved like a horn as he thrust his chin continually forwards. His heavy, wrinkled lids gave his small eyes the look of those of an ageing mastiff. He wore an expensive-looking tie tucked into his surgeon's white coat, and showy cuff links of gold and mother-of-pearl in the sleeves of the shirt he wore beneath it.

'Welcome to our institution, inspector!' he said, ushering Salazar into the bare room, which looked more like a mortuary than an office. The furniture was that of a consulting room. Steel and plastic, also pale brown in colour, like the lino. The glass doors to the two little cupboards to either side of the desk were engraved with Hippocrates' serpent. A huge black wooden crucifix hung on the end wall. Salazar sat down in one of the two small armchairs flanking a small glass table on which stood a relief model of the hospital. The doctor sat down in the other, opening his white coat to reveal a grey double-breasted jacket.

'Your superiors have informed me of your mission. Obviously, you can count on my total collaboration. We cannot be everywhere at once, inspector! And I know that the angels of death have infiltrated this hospital, as they have so many others. We are for ever vigilant, but that is not enough. Two years ago we arrested several abortionists who were making contact with their clients in our clinic. We reported the suspects and asked the police to carry out surprise inspections of our doctors' premises and equipment. But more than that we cannot do!'

Salazar looked around him. He noted the tidy desk, its glass top immaculate; a photograph of a seaside villa in a silver frame, the doctor's shoes, their soles still completely unmarked by use, the expensive fountain pen in the pocket of his white coat. He sensed that the man was a typical high-ranking civil servant, cut out for receptions and gala evenings rather than for detective work.

'I quite understand, doctor. I'm here to give you a hand in just such matters. Tell me more about how the palliative care unit functions.'

'The patients in that unit, as you know, have meagre chances of recovery. Their survival is in the hands of God in all His infinite mercy. So the only treatment they receive is the therapy of prayer, as indeed do all patients struck down by fatal illnesses before their cases become terminal.'

'So, even before they come into the palliative care unit, you are already able to tell which patients have no faith in such therapy.'

22

'Unfortunately, euthaniasists cannot be identified at this early stage. When a patient realizes that he has been stricken by a fatal illness, his natural reaction is to rebel against his fate. Prayer therapy serves to help him to resign himself and we have scientific proof that it can perform miracles, if scrupulously carried out. In this field, papal medicine is progressing by leaps and bounds. As you will know, a miracle occurs over three stages: predisposition, acceptance and accomplishment. Many of our patients get as far as acceptance, which is when clear signs of recovery appear. But lack of faith prevents them from entering the accomplishment phase. Of course, in such cases the collective prayers of other patients for those of their companions who have reached the state of acceptance would be extremely helpful; but human pettiness knows no bounds. One sick man does not willingly pray to save another. Governed by selfishness, he prays with a lie in his heart; God senses as much and lets them both decline. And this is just punishment for one who refuses to love his neighbour as himself. But, as I have said, we are studying the phenomenon of the miracle, and we are now in a position to give it something of a helping hand. We have discovered that intense prayer is at its most effective when the phase of predisposition is drawing to a close. The most recent research into the miracles performed by our saints is telling us that there is a hierarchy of grace. In other words, specific cures require the intercession of specific saints. It is no use doing what we Italians so often do, namely turn to those divine figures whom we love the most, for instance the Virgin Mary, regarding them as more influential. For centuries now the Church has been conducting a series of finely-tuned experiments proving that divine figures too much called upon tend to withdraw, to become more elusive. This is quite understandable: too much divine intervention would upset the balance between the prospect of salvation and the credibility of the Last Judgement. In a word, God cannot save us until the time is ripe. That is why turning to the saints, particularly in their areas of expertise, may be more effective. Furthermore, here we come upon yet another example of the wisdom of the Church, which has always pointed to the saints as examples of thorough-going humanity achieved through faith. This line of research is also leading to a heightened understanding of any one saint's specific powers. To give a concrete example: nothing is more effective for the curing of a tumour on the breast than praying to Saint Agatha.'

Trying to conceal his impatience, Salazar heard him out.

'I see. So, to go back to the more concrete side of my enquiries, can you confirm that the only effective route to catching a dying man bent on euthanasia is via his family?'

'Undoubtedly. We have also had some arrested by allowing corrupt doctors to catch them in flagrante. But the price to be paid in human lives is too high for this to be a valid strategy. To catch a euthanasiast doctor, we have to allow him to kill too many patients. And that, from the point of view of our doctrine, is a cost that is not sustainable.'

Before continuing, the doctor leant towards Salazar, covered his mouth with his hand and whispered:

'Even if, between the two of us, in the crusade against the Cathars, Arnold of Citeaux was not altogether in the wrong when he said: 'Kill the lot of them. God will recognize his own!'

Having uttered these words, the doctor fell back into his chair with a malicious smile. Salazar looked away, lost in thought. He folded his hands and lifted them to his chin.

'And how do you respond when you identify a terminally-ill patient who is hoping to have recourse to euthanasia?'

'The first thing we do is to get him to confess. That way, at least his soul will be saved. Then we report the members of his family, and here justice and the law intervene. As you know, the punishment may vary: from fines to expropriation of property, down to excommunication and the loss of civil rights. But this does not concern us, inspector. We are on the battlefield, counting the dead and wounded!' explained the doctor, waving his goatee.

'Just one last thing – how do you get a euthanasiast to confess? Excuse my curiosity, but I've been living abroad for years and I no longer know how things are done in Italy. I need to know as much as possible, to understand the mentality of those I'm dealing with.' Salazar did not expect to benefit much from this conversation, but he felt something might be gained by keeping on the right side of the man.

'Oh, I quite understand, inspector! That's what I'm here for! And you're quite right – confession is not something that can be enforced. It has to come from the heart. So we encourage it with persuasion. While he is still conscious, and not as yet too weakened by illness, we see to it that the patient has regular sessions with our psychologists, apparently "free-ranging" conversations which provide an outlet for him to express his fear, whereas for us they offer a window on to his state of mind. If these are not sufficient, we organize catechism sessions and obligatory prayer vigils for the patient and his family. It is often these which make him see the error of his ways, if not out of faith, then at least for form's sake. As you may know, the law is more lenient with the relatives of a confessed criminal.'

'Most interesting. What you have told me has given me a better idea of how to proceed,' said Salazar, as though thinking aloud. The doctor was now gazing at him absently, as though his mind were elsewhere.

'Inspector, do you believe in guardian angels?' he asked a little hesitantly.

Salazar paused before answering. 'Of course I do! As number 328 of Joseph Ratzinger's catechism puts it, *angels are individual beings endowed with intelligence and will*,' was his prudent reply, when it finally came.

'Don't misunderstand me, I'm not trying to pry, nor do I doubt your faith. I know that practical men like you have no time to linger over such subtleties. But today we papal scientists, who are used to peering into the mysteries of creation, are giving new importance to these beings which Ratzinger's catechism describes as *purely spiritual beings, incorporeal, invisible and immortal*. We are beginning to believe that this invisibility and incorporeality may not preclude a certain contact with the human world. Recent research in our department of parapsychology has discovered methods of making contact with guardian angels – with techniques derived from hypnotism, comparable to a mystic's ecstasy. Simply put, by means of an induced trance, the human mind can discern the wavelength on which guardian angels communicate, a bit like tuning into a radio station whose frequency is normally imperceptible to the human ear. Here, though, it is the soul which does the tuning. Such practices must be conducted with caution, however, since this same frequency is also that used by demons. But, despite the risk, it is still worth a try. Our researchers have made contact with certain wingless angels, who are the easiest to reach because they are present on earth in considerable numbers. It is in this area that we may be of some assistance to you – by seeking to make contact with the guardian angels of the terminally ill. They are certainly in a position to tell us what is going on in their protégés' hearts and minds. Obviously, we need time, and you would have to undergo specific training.' The doctor had now assumed the air of someone who is giving a diagnosis and prescribing a cure. He bit his lip, and his goatee shot forwards as he did so.

'Thanks for the suggestion, doctor. I'll mention it to my superiors, though I doubt that my task will leave me time for training of this kind. But it may be a path to consider in the future,' said Salazar, getting himself off the hook, he felt, with some adroitness.

'As you prefer, inspector. We are at your service!' replied the doctor, making an expansive gesture. Salazar nodded courteously. He could hardly wait to get out of the room.

'I have no more questions for the moment, but if it's not too much trouble I shall be back when I know more about the patients. One last thing. Do I have your permission to look at your doctors' personal files?' That was the only thing he really wanted to ask. The doctor raised a hand to his chin, and a large watch emerged from his shirt cuff as he did so.

'Unfortunately we have no access to such files except in the case of explicit charges. For preliminary inquiries we need authorization from the Papal Medical Council, as required by professional ethics. Suspicion of our doctors would amount to lack of faith in the system. You will have to ask your superior about such matters. But I am sure that a secret agent in the papal force will have no difficulty in procuring a piece of paper with a couple of official stamps, inspector! Ah, bureaucratic procedure, what a thing it is! How could we live without it!' exclaimed the doctor, rising elegantly from his chair to offer Salazar his hand. The inspector freed himself from the man's sweaty grasp as quickly as he decently could, and left the room, after yet more thanks, received by their grim recipient with a series of goatee-waggles, in lieu of more orthodox leave-taking.

Throughout the day, a leaden sky had seemed to promise snow; the nearby Monti Prenestini were already sprinkled with white. But in the evening the rain returned and the radio announced that the Tiber might flood during the night. Salazar had spent his first days studying the patients' files. In subsequent meetings, the vicar had given him the abstracts from the Land Registry concerning all relevant properties, and the police files on all the patients' close relatives. The inspector now knew the personal histories of each of the men who were dying in the palliative care unit. He had started cross-referencing the data, seeking points of connection. Documentation on the doctors would have provided him with other pointers; but the inspector did not like too much paperwork. This was not a game to be played in the archives. He was going to have to get out on the street, find a trail and follow it. He had immediately discarded the atheists among the twenty-seven patients: they would be easy quarry. Those who declare themselves have nothing to hide. Instead, he concentrated on those who had survived the longest. It was they who were the most tempted to put an end to it all. Whichever of them was Davide Zago, he must have accomplices who were pretending to be his relatives and coming to pay him visits. There couldn't be many people providing this cover. He therefore discarded those who had a lot of registered visitors. He was now left with five potential suspects. That Thursday, he waited until it was time for the evening visit, then took the corridor to the palliative care unit.

The whole of the first floor of that wing of the hospital was occupied by patients who were terminally ill. The windows overlooked the inner courtyards of the building, and the entrances to the various storerooms and depots. Above, on the flat roof, the back of a large lit-up sign saying 'San Filippo Neri' was visible, supported by rusty posts stuck in the concrete. The windowless prayer room was situated between the unit's two corridors. By day it received a little feeble light from the two frosted glass doors which gave on to the outer wing of the building, which itself could not be reached from that same floor. It was there that the first corridor ended. The second one opened off to the left of the prayer room and continued around the edge of the courtyard.

In the first room there were two beds, the faces of their occupants, who showed no sign of movement, carved out by the dim white glow of the nightlight. Their breathing seemed to divide the narrow space into two parts: it sounded like whispered voices, trying to persuade anyone who would listen of some enormous truth. On the side of the room where the door was, it was the first – soft and phlegm-laden – which was the stronger. On the window side the breathing was dry and rasping, often breaking up into bursts of intermittent coughing. In the middle of the room both were equally audible. Despite their different rhythms, they sometimes coincided, could briefly be heard as one, then once again diverged. Like two nightbirds, they vanished and reappeared, flew suddenly downwards and soared up again. A woman was seated by the bed on the window side, her head bent, one hand on the sick man's arm, the other telling her beads. Salazar went up to her. He glanced at the hand that was lying on the sheet, at the big black veins pierced by the needles from the drip, at the catheter tube dripping into the bag hanging from the edge of the bed. The man's eyes were half-closed, but he was looking upwards, his open mouth almost lipless. When the woman turned in his direction, Salazar nodded his head and pointed to the crucifix on his jacket. The woman nodded and went back to her prayers. In the meantime the other patient's visitor had also arrived. He was a big man, probably around forty. Without taking off his coat, he stood at the foot of the bed and shuffled his feet on the floor. He was holding his hat in one hand, and occasionally wiping the sweat from his forehead with the other; his expression, as he looked at the man he was visiting, was somewhere between surprise and dismay. He had a parcel of fresh linen with him, and handed it to the sister, eager to be rid of it. He cannot have been a regular visitor, because when he saw Salazar he made as though to offer him his chair. Salazar communicated his refusal by gestures, raising his hand and half-closing his eyes. Then he slipped out of the room; it had no more to tell him. He went into the next one, where the light was on, and a soundless television was sending out blue flashes over the steel of the bed frames. A man was sitting at a table near the window, holding a newspaper in place with his crooked elbows. For a moment Salazar wondered if he were crying, but the man looked up at him for a moment, dry-eyed, then carried on reading. The man in the next bed had tubes in his nose; the silence was broken by a slight gurgling sound, not unlike that of deep-sea diving equipment. The other bed, the one next to the door, was empty. Salazar carried on down the corridor to complete his pious rounds. He wanted to get this mission over and done with as soon as possible so that he could get back to Amsterdam. But at the same time he felt a morbid curiosity about this world of pain. On his way back to the sister's office, he found himself in the prayer room. He sat down on a bench to take stock of things. The room was in semi-darkness; the only light came from the glass partition giving on to the corridor of the adjacent ward, spreading over the bubbles in the linoleum and turning them into dim puddles of whiteness. The little cupboard which served as an altar had been pushed up against the wall, the benches stacked up at the end of the room. The crucifix and the embroidery on the chaplain's vestments, folded on top of a large missal, glistened faintly in the half-light. A radiator was ticking, the flow of hot water through its pipes making a soft murmuring sound which filled the silence. Suddenly the door to the other ward was opened; two white-coated doctors appeared and immediately locked the door behind them. They came forward cautiously, the soles of their shoes flattening the bubbles on the linoleum, their shadows splintered by the dazzling lamplight. They were engaged in lively argument, although they kept their voices down. One was shaking his head, while the other kept on saying: 'I can't do it, I just can't! Not now!' They had not noticed Salazar, who was standing in a recess, the upper part of his body sunk in shadow, his legs hidden by a pile of chairs. It was only when they were well into the room that the two doctors saw him, and instantly fell silent, greeted him coldly and went off. Salazar waited until their silhouettes had vanished down the corridor, then, mingling with the relatives who were coming out of the wards, laden with piles of dirty linen and redoubled anguish, he went slowly back to the sister's office.

'Sister, what time do you close the gate to the unit?'

'At eight o'clock, straight after supper. That's when the night-watch starts.'

'Do you close all the doors? Including those which lead to the other wing?'

'Those are never open.'

'Aha! Not even in the day?'

'Well, they're no longer in use, you see. We have the keys,

though.'

Salazar smiled to himself. He had already found the flaw.

'So no one can get in without coming through here?' he asked, as though to spell things out.

'The duty nurse is the only one who can open up. This is the command button.' The nurse pointed to an electric panel set into the wall of the porter's lodge.

'And how does the night-watch get in and out?'

'They have to come through our porter's lodge. There's an intercom system for emergencies.'

The sister was about to leave. She switched off the computer, lowered the blinds and seemed about to leave the office.

'Signor Salazar, if you want to stay here for the vigils, I've put a camp-bed in the space behind the changing-rooms. That way you'll be able to get to the bathroom more easily and no one will disturb you,' she said, giving him a knowing look.

'Thank you, sister,' he said in a neutral tone.

'Good night then!' Attaching the bunch of keys to her belt, she slipped on her black jacket and set off towards the stairs.

'Good night!' Salazar went with her for a few paces, pretending to be lost in thought. He paused on the gallery to observe the comings and goings of the staff as they ended their shift. When it seemed to him that the way was clear, he went quickly back into the prayer room, pulled the cupboard holding the altar under the video-surveillance camera, climbed on to it and trained the lens on to the door through which the two doctors had gone. Then he went to lie down on his camp-bed, took off his shoes and folded the cushion beneath his head. From where he lay he had a view of the screens in the sister's office, the way into the corridor and the entrance to the stairs. The new duty nurse had switched on the neon lighting and settled into her seat in the porter's lodge, the blue of her freshly ironed nurse's uniform clearly visible in the darkness as she poured herself a hot drink from a thermos. She gave Salazar a vacant look and opened her newspaper out on the table.

Kept awake by the patients' moans, Salazar spent a sleepless night. He timed the movements of the night-watch, the comings and goings of the lifts, even the movements of the buses in the street below. He kept his eye on the video-surveillance system in the prayer room and on the occasionally nodding head of the nurse in the porter's lodge. From time to time he glanced at the clock on the wall, noting the all too slow passing of the hours. He saw the traffic on the avenue thinning out, and the last empty train on the overground slipping over the railway bridge. At seven on the dot the night-watch went off duty and the nurses on the new shift started pushing the medicine trolleys along the corridor. Salazar folded up his bedclothes, closed up the camp-bed and went into the bathroom to wash his face. He met the new sister on the stairs; she was out of breath, and her cheeks were pink with cold.

'Up already, father? At least come and have a coffee. Real coffee, not that stuff from the machines. We nurses have our own mocha, and I've brought some croissants!' she said, pointing to the bag on her arm.

'Thank you, sister, but I'm in a bit of a hurry,' he said, and scuttled off down the steps. Outside, the wind had got up again. He breathed in the damp air with a sense of relief; after a night spent with the smell of warm plastic and disinfectant in his nostrils, even the stench of diesel from the buses on the square was welcome. He didn't feel like joining in the rough and tumble of the overground quite yet, and decided to walk on to the next stop. Once he got on, he soon dozed off, and was awoken by a sudden jolt just before the bridge over the Tiber. In front of the convent, the newspaper kiosk was already open. He bought a copy of the *Osservatore Romano* and went up to his room, where he filled his pipe, lit the table lamp, opened the newspaper and, taking his first puff, read the front page headline: 'Death penalty for abortionists'.

*Yesterday at the Angelus the Holy Father once again called for those found guilty of abortion, whether practitioners or advocates, to suffer the death penalty. By so doing, the Pope is giving his explicit support to the Ministry of Justice of the Italian Catholic Republic, which has already proposed a similar law on two occasions. As is well-known, the proposal was both times rejected with an adverse vote by the Justice Board of rank and file Catholics. Their ideological tenacity has been repeatedly criticized by their own allies in the government, but to no avail. Today, many observers are wondering what credence can be given to a movement which is now politically isolated, and which is adopting a position of questionable theological severity in defence of the enemies of the Church. The essence of Faith does not lend itself to succinct interpretations, but is nonetheless crystal clear, as the Holy Father has emphasized over the last few days. Buoyed up by the arrest, last month, of yet another unit of backstreet abortionist doctors, the government is now launching a new offensive to storm the last bastions of recalcitrance, and hence to endow our country with this invaluable juridical instrument for the defence of all our citizens. Monsignor Damiani has already drafted a third bill. It is to be hoped that on this occasion the rank and file Catholics will give their support to this long-awaited measure. Number 2267 of Joseph Ratzinger's catechism of the Catholic Church reads as follows: "Always supposing that the identity and responsibility of the guilty party have been fully established, the traditional teaching of the Church does not exclude recourse to the death penalty, if this is the only feasible way of defending the lives of human beings against such unjust aggression." The events of the last few weeks prove that our society is now in precisely such an emergency situation as that described by Joseph Ratzinger. The abortionist criminals are striking at human life at its most vulnerable, that is, within the mother's womb. Thus Benedict XVIII's appeal for fitting punishment is in complete conformity with a well-established doctrinal approach which should find favour amongst all the faithful. "The rank and file Catholics' vetoing of a law which safeguards human life is incomprehensible, and their position within the government must now be questioned," Monsignor Damiani firmly stated recently. Today much of the heat seems to have gone out of the argument, all the more so because the government can apparently rely on a majority to get the law through without calling upon the rank and file Catholics. "We wish to avoid pointless friction within the majority but we cannot betray the hopes of the electors who have given us their votes," said Monsignor Damiani, mindful of the fact that if the rank and file Catholics left the government on a matter of doctrine, this might raise doubts about the movement's legality. But opinion polls conducted by* Ecclesia *show that the rank and file Catholic movement is crumbling. "It is disheartening to note that opposition to this government, with the exception of the exemplary case of the Christian Democrats, is continually dominated by subversive and anti-Catholic fringe parties which the state has no option but to declare illegal for its own protection," said the Minister of Justice on Radio Maria.*

Salazar turned out the light, put his pipe down on the bedside table and watched the coils of smoke wreathing upwards in the semi-darkness until he fell asleep.

Looking them in the eye aroused even more revulsion. That is, if you could locate their eyes in the yellow masks of those faces distorted by suffering. But Salazar was a hound of God, and he did not flinch. He learned to recognize them. From 148 to 152. His 'set of five', he called them, as in bingo. Inevitably, he also felt compassion for them, though he tried to keep it in check, in order to allow his soul to be totally taken over by suspicion. He must not put his trust in those expressionless faces, those livid hunks of flesh now barely stirring amidst the chill whiteness of the sheets. They were not often awake, so Salazar found himself having to make a tour of the dark rooms more than once. He would pause whenever he caught somebody's eye. He could not always be certain they had seen him; he would show them the crucifix and sit down by the bed. The 'conversations' he had with them were largely silent, conducted by means of signs, brief gestures before they lapsed back into sleep, uttering faint groans which sometimes sounded like strangled laughter. Some tried to talk to him: they spoke of matters of little importance, asking him to move something on the bedside table, to give them a glass of water, which they would not be able to hold, or to look for their slippers under the bed, slippers they had not worn for days or weeks, and which the cleaner had put on the chair when she mopped the floor. Their fear seemed dimmed by some even greater worry which was theirs alone, and which they did not seek to share. In their moments of wakefulness they looked around them as though uncertain where they were, almost irritated by the voices and shadows which distracted them from their calvary. They had work to do, they had no time to spare to listen to pious relatives or cooperate with wretched nurses offering pointless pills.

'Sister, could you tell me which of these five are still taking medication?' That evening Salazar had arrived with a bee in his bonnet. He had separated some files out from the rest, and now he put them down on the desk.

'Let me just check,' said the sister, turning the computer screen in her direction.

'I particularly want to know who's being given morphine,' he added.

'All except 148.'

'Doesn't he need it?'

'He's already been given the regulation amount. It's a rule. The patients need to bear witness to Christ's suffering on the cross...' the nurse explained, as though reciting something by rote.

'Of course', murmured Salazar, running a hand thoughtfully through his hair. At that same moment he saw the woman from the evening before, going towards the exit. She was wearing a blue handkerchief tied beneath her chin, with a tuft of fair hair protruding from it on to her forehead. She was a hard-featured woman, with narrow eyes above high cheekbones. She walked with a firm, proud step, as though powered by some secret rage. One hand was in her pocket, the other on the strap of her shoulder bag. Salazar opened the file of patient 148: Marco Bonardi lived at Via Cornelia 327, in Monte Spaccato. He was looked after by his daughter Chiara.

It was he, no. 148, who seemed the most alert. One afternoon Salazar had found him propped up on his elbows, apparently looking out of the window. The nurse came up to lie him down flat on his back again, explaining to Salazar that it was spasms of pain that caused him to adopt that unusual pose. Sometimes he would talk out loud, eyes wide open, but empty, staring out on to the darkness of delirium. Yet every so often it seemed to Salazar that those eyes would flash – in alarm, perhaps – as though he had recognized him as someone he knew. He was the old man who was visited by the woman with the rosary. All in all, Salazar was more suspicious of her than of him. He'd kept a close eye on her, evening after evening. Her grief was somehow too self-assured; too falsely spontaneous, allowing the onlooker to sense a certain calculated detachment even in the way she said her prayers. Nor did the rosary she handled so distractedly look right in her hands: they were fine hands, educated hands, which seemed almost to think when they touched things or tucked that tuft of rebellious fair hair back into her handkerchief. Because he had to start somewhere, the inspector decided to find out more about Chiara Bonardi.

The next evening, the woman seemed to be waiting for him at the vending machine on the ground floor; or at least she didn't immediately move away when she saw him approaching. She was sipping a cappuccino, warming her hands on the hot plastic beaker. Visiting time was just over. The relatives were filing out, a silent crowd of them thronging the entrance hall with its artificial plants. A smell of cooking wafted along the corridors. Salazar went up to the vending machine, put in a coin and pressed the button for an espresso.

'Good evening, might I have a word?'

'By all means.'

'Our paths crossed some days ago. I am a pilgrim priest. I'm in charge of the patients in the palliative care unit.'

'I know,' she said quickly, hiding her mouth behind her

beaker.

'We hold prayer vigils, we help the sisters and give a general hand with the running of the place.'

The woman nodded, a flicker of impatience visible on her face.

'I know what a pilgrim priest is,' she said with a strained smile, as though trying to be polite. She looked at the crucifix on Salazar's jacket.

'We are also here to help the families. We know that these are difficult times. But life must go on, and there are so many problems. Is there anything that I can do for you? Have you children who need collecting from school? Elderly relatives who need looking after? Anything else that I could do?'

'No thanks, I have no children. And father has lived alone for many years.'

With the yellow ochre light from the streetlamps filtering in through the glazed doors, the modern building looked more than ever like an industrial hangar.

'Please, if you're busy, don't let me keep you.'

'No, that's all right. It's been a long day, I'm just having a hot drink before going out again. Tomorrow I shan't have time to come and see my father,' she said, swallowing the last drop.

'I hear they've stopped giving him morphine,' Salazar ventured to say.

'Those are the rules,' she answered sharply.

'Is he eating?'

'He has the odd teaspoonful of water. Then there's the drip...'

'It could be a long business...'

'We are in the hands of God,' the woman broke in as though she wanted to end the matter. Then she sighed, long and deeply, and started looking around nervously for something in the distance on which she could focus her attention.

'Perhaps it would be better to let them die…' said Salazar suggestively, his eyes on the woman's face. She pressed her lips together and looked quickly back at him.

'But that's just what we're doing, isn't it?' she said in a low voice. Then she threw the plastic beaker into the bin, smiled coldly and walked away, knotting her blue handkerchief firmly under her chin. Salazar waited a moment or two before going up the stairs. He looked at his watch: a quarter past seven. He ran up to the first floor, took his coat from the coatrack in the sister's office and went back down to the entrance hall. He had no difficulty in spotting the blue handkerchief among the other heads walking towards the door. There were few people in the overground station. The train coming from Labaro was already pulling in. Salazar hurried on to the platform and just managed to slip into a carriage at the last minute. Chiara Bonardi was seated a few feet away, with her back to him, staring blankly into the middle distance. The lights of Torrevecchia skittered over the train windows. Beneath the flyover the streets all looked the same, with their rows of red and yellow lights, and the windows of the blocks of flats which the train almost seemed to be running into when the railway curved. Still unraised shutters revealed kitchens and living rooms, televisions, corridors and stairs. Salazar looked idly at the headlines in other people's newspapers. The river Aniene had burst its banks and flooded the railway at Monte Mario; there was a crush at the station on Via Boccea. Chiara Bonardi was now moving towards the door. Salazar waited for her to get out before doing so himself. He followed her through the puddles of a car park in front of a supermarket, then along a road which ran beside a building site. She then went into a wider street which was better lit, and full of traffic. Salazar followed her at a prudent distance, checking his whereabouts on his handheld sat nav. They were a few hundred metres away from what he knew to be her home address. Via Cornelia was the next on the right. The woman crossed the street, stopped in front of the window of a bar and went towards a low, wide block of flats in the middle of a row of garages. She walked up the steps, stopped to look for her keys in her bag and disappeared into the entrance hall. Salazar waited for a moment before going up to check the bells: Bonardi, fourth floor, staircase B. He looked at his watch: it was eight forty-four.

That evening, when he got back to the Carmelite Convent, it seemed to him that someone had searched his room. Nothing was missing, his pipe was in its place, as was his diary. But somehow it was not quite as he had left it, Salazar was sure of that. He ran his hand over the door posts and the top of the cupboard: strangely, there was not a speck of dust. He inspected the lamp, the backs of the chairs and the bathroom cupboard in search of bugging equipment but found nothing. Still harbouring a lingering suspicion, he sat down as the table and began to write.

*Atheist is a catch-all term. If you have grown up among churches, you are not the same sort of atheist as you would be if you'd grown up among mosques. Everyone is an atheist in terms of their own God. Some religions guard against atheism better than others; Protestantism, for example, fairly welcomes it in. Anyone who has been capable of contesting one set of dogma will not accept another; and anyone who starts to think rationally about God will be an atheist. But atheism will not be eliminated by persecuting atheists. It is the sons who have to be targeted, the fathers are already lost.*

*That is why, in Holland, we have forged an alliance with the imams. We are experimenting with mixed services, studying the psalms and the suras together, though unbeknownst to the powers that be, for obvious reasons. For them, everything is a matter of outward form. They would not understand; indeed, I would be in trouble if they found out. For the moment I have to act in secret, but time will prove me right. The old generation of theologians will be swept aside by the new priests of Bible-koranism. The powers that be cannot conceive of such a phenomenon; they will become aware of it only when it is already rampant. This is the new frontier of globalized faith. The churches which will survive will be those which stand firm against competition in the new market of religions. If they do not want to be swept away by the new forms of evangelism, the new sects, and scientism, our leaders must accept change. Furthermore, this is the only possible future: the three religions of the book must make common cause. No one will have any difficulty acknowledging the Pope of Rome when there is just one faith. But in order to bring about this revolution, we must start now. We must make our presence felt in schools, in the street, through all manner of networks and associations. A westerner who goes into a mosque is a triumph for us too. He has become a believer, he has set reason aside. No religion is better than Islam at cloaking faith in reason. Muslims use reason to reveal the intelligent order which pervades creation, and that is the way to disarm science. We stand around wrangling over the sacraments and women priests; we can't agree on anything, not even on the emblem of the cross. They simply kneel down beneath the crescent and then all pray in the same way. I observed our atheists during lauds. There they are, dressed up as believers for decency's sake, possibly even with a rosary in their hand. The Church makes do with appearances. It is far too long since it inspired martyrdom.*

That Friday the vicar's black shoes were already on the footstool when Salazar went into the church of Sant'Andrea della Valle. He kneeled down before the confessional, which already smelled of mouthwash.

'Vicar, I need to gain access to the personal files of the doctors in the palliative care unit,' he said without further preamble.

'Identify yourself, my son,' came the cold answer from the other side of the grille. Salazar patiently recited the Credo and then gave his registration number, as procedure required.

'You cannot afford to skimp on such matters, inspector! You never know who might be seated on this chair! Even today the abortionists threatened the Holy See with new manifestos: posters extolling the secular revolution have been stuck up on the Leonine Walls, no less. Now speak on.'

'Vicar, I need to consult the files on the doctors in the hospital. I was told to ask you for your permission.'

'I will give authorization to the Guardian of the Faith at San Filippo Neri and send you copies of all the files you wish to see. Are there any other developments?'

'Nothing as yet, vicar. I have identified several suspects and am making enquiries. The hospital is not as closed a world as I had imagined.'

'I thought as much. We have been dropping our guard for quite some time. In a way this helps us lay our trap. So, play your cards well and reveal yourself only when the moment to strike has come.'

'Maybe you're right. We've dropped our guard,' Salazar concurred. Then he crossed himself, stood up from the prie-dieu and walked off down the nave.

Chiara Bonardi left the flat at seven on the dot to go to eight o'clock mass at the hospital. Those relatives who did not attend mass regularly, and register their entry at the turnstile, lost the subsidy for palliative care and had to pay the hospital out of their own pockets.

Salazar had already been sitting in the bar opposite for a good half hour. He waited until she had turned the corner, then paid for his coffee and walked towards the block.

The flat was clean and tidy. A crucifix with an olive branch hung on the wall of the hall above the mirror on the coatrack. He went through the pockets of the coat which was hanging there, and found receipts from a hairdresser's and a beauty salon. He noted the addresses: Via dei Gracchi and Via Silla. Odd, he thought, they're right in the city centre, a long way away from Monte Spaccato. He folded them up and put them in his pocket. The furniture was old, but well-kept.

In the red-tiled kitchen, a smell of coffee lingered. The main bedroom, with its double bed, was clearly never used; the mattress was covered with an embroidered bedspread which was too short for it, and the stitching was fraying here and there. The lamps on the bedside tables were unplugged. The cupboard was empty, apart from a man's summer jacket and a battered Panama hat. Another little room, leading into the bathroom, contained an ironing-board, a clothes rack, a shoe cupboard and a laundry basket; bottles of water, a few packets of pasta, some jars of jam and two packets of washing powder stood on a nearby shelf.

Chiara Bonardi's room must be the one at the end of the corridor, Salazar thought to himself. That room at least showed signs of being lived in: a pair of pyjamas thrown over a chair, a cup of tisane on the bedside table, the duvet pulled up over the pillow. The main item of furniture in the living room was a large green leather divan; the parquet flooring was worn but well polished, and under the television a few blocks had come loose. On the table there was a vase of dried flowers, yesterday's paper and a season ticket for the underground, in the name of Chiara Bonardi. The books in the shelves were meticulously arranged by height, forming uniform waves which seemed carved into the wood: adventure stories, history books, travelogues and a row of geology manuals alternated with primitive statuettes and other relics. Some handles on the dresser had been replaced with other, almost identical ones, distinguishable from the originals only by the brightness of the brass. The walls were hung with framed photographs of oilfields, Bedouin on camels, tanned-looking men at the wheels of jeeps. Marco Bonardi had been a mining engineer; he had spent his life travelling the world extracting oil for ENI. Salazar pulled open a few drawers where, among piles of CDs and letters, he found four photograph albums.

He took them into the kitchen, laid them on the table and began leafing through them. The images they contained were of two interconnected families; they had been assembled with considerable care, with dates and comments, so as to tell a coherent story. Even without knowing him, Salazar soon identified Marco Bonardi, and was amused to see him ageing from one album to the next, while the little girl who was playing around him on the beach in the first album was becoming a young woman. In photos of her with her women friends, Chiara was always the tallest; she seemed to be the leader. She was more obviously recognizable in the fourth album, where Marco Bonardi featured only rarely, alongside a sweet-faced woman who must have been his wife. In the last pages the photos ranged more widely over time. They showed a now

45

adult Chiara Bonardi on a flower-filled terrace, and then on a beach with a woman friend. Here a sun-tanned Marco Bonardi now appeared again, in shirt-sleeves, in front of a monument, or in exotic landscapes, with palms and minarets. There were also several portrait studies, taken in an interior which seemed to be this very flat. Carefully, Salazar detached one and slipped it into his pocket. The smallest album was half empty, with just a few poorly framed shots of landscapes, small figures, the first floors of anonymous houses, a car groaning with luggage, a lit Christmas tree. There were no longer any dates, or commentaries; it was as though the painstaking hand which had organized the earlier albums had suddenly grown weary of the task. Outside, a pale sun was emerging through the smoky sky. Salazar looked gloomily at the shadows of the shutters as they lengthened on the wall. He put everything back in place and was already at the door when he realized that something about those photographs didn't quite add up. He looked at the one he had removed from the album, running his fingers over the back and edges. He went back into the living room, leafed through the last album and then reopened it, starting at the end. It was then that he noticed that some of the photos were fixed in with adhesive corner-pieces, while others were glued straight on to the page. He detached a couple of them, more brightly coloured than the rest. The paper, too, was different, coated with plastic, and thinner. They all bore the same date on the back, stamped faintly on the margins, a date in December of the previous year.

The following evening, he waited for the woman in front of the vending machine. He had bought himself a coffee, just to have something in his hands, but he didn't feel like drinking it.

'We seem to keep the same hours!' he said when he saw her

approaching, though she was clearly eager to be off.

'My timetable is dictated by necessity,' she said, keeping her hands in her pockets, as though resigned to enduring Salazar's company. The inspector promptly produced a coin.

'What are you drinking?'

'A cappuccino, thanks.' The machine placed a plastic beaker in the ring and a puff of warm froth emerged from the spout.

'How are things?' asked Salazar, nodding in the direction of the stairs to the palliative care unit.

'Same as ever. I can't be sure whether he is conscious or not. At times I feel that he hears what I'm saying, that he knows I'm there. Then he seems to drift away. Sometimes I think he's stupefied by pain. He's got absolutely no strength, he can hardly breath. All we can do is wait...' The woman had her patter at the ready. It was best to be on the alert. That man too might be a Guardian of the Faith, they were poking their noses into everything nowadays. Particularly in hospitals; and if they reported you, that was that.

'But he's alive! And while there's life, there's hope!' exclaimed Salazar with a pious simper.

'We are in the hands of God,' she concluded resignedly, lifting the plastic beaker to her lips.

'Signora Bonardi, you mustn't worry, I am not the person you think I am. I know the feelings of those who are watching a loved one die. All thoughts are legitimate in such cases. The Church too understands this, and our role as pilgrim priests is precisely to accept the believer's doubts in these difficult moments. That is why we are independent of the church hierarchy, and accountable to no one,' said Salazar mendaciously, drawing the woman aside. Years of experience with unbelievers had turned him into an artful preacher. But putting yourself on the side of those whom you wish to convert had always been rule number one with priests and salesmen. Chiara Bonardi was no simpleton. She knew that she must proceed with care, particularly during this fateful vigil.

'Father, I have no doubts. I am certain that my father will be going to heaven. With what he's suffering, he deserves to.' She put her hands back in her pockets, nodded in his direction and walked off. Salazar stood there staring after her. He hadn't yet decided whether she was putting on an act, or whether she was perfectly sincere. Leaving his coffee untouched, he went up the stairs. The duty nurse was already at her post, the newspaper open in front of her. Salazar opened up his camp-bed and threw on the cover. He checked the monitors in the sister's office. He saw the doctor with the goatee emerging from the main corridor, wearing a flashy coat with a fur collar and toying with a ridiculous hat resembling a busby, which he clearly could not quite bring himself to put on.

*I am beginning to be intrigued by these euthanasiasts and all their works. Here we have another example of science taking a wrong turn. Science had hoped to make man live for ever, but in fact all it does is make him die more slowly. Things were better when we knew less, when diseases were incurable, when heart attacks and tumours felled us at a blow. Death is easier when it is unforeseen. The world lived in peace until it rediscovered Greek thought and, with it, the mania for experiment. To experiment means ceasing to put one's trust in the created world, but wanting to take it apart. This is another of the manias that science brings in its wake. Now our task must be to bury knowledge. To forget it. To cut off connections between scientists, to spread error, to lead people down the wrong track. In Rome, no one is aware of the awesome battle we are fighting outside the Catholic world. Two years ago in London a scientist at Imperial College killed himself. The news went unreported in the Italian press. Neil Corrigan was doing research into mirror neurons. His work had reached a point where he could prove that men and animals have very much in common in terms of feelings. He was in a position to prove that all earthly life is moved by an invisible empathy, and this is tantamount to pantheism. They ordered us to kill him. We did more than they could have hoped: we falsified his calculations, making him appear a charlatan in the eyes of the scientific community. So, out of sheer desperation, he did the job for us, and killed himself, throwing his research into total discredit as he did so. Our fight, therefore, must be to demolish science. In Africa, we intercept anti-AIDS vaccines and replace them with ampoules containing water. The illness is spreading, and man is losing faith in science; he is beginning to understand that God is the stronger of the two. In the Indian sub-continent we sterilize the seed provided by international food aid and reduce millions to starvation, so that they will emigrate to the West and become easy prey. Such are the battles we are waging.*

Salazar put down his pen for a moment. He took the postcard of Veere from his exercise-book and turned it over in his hands, wondering how Guntur was getting on. He had tried to ring him from a public call box the previous day and left a message on the answer machine, but there had been no reply. He turned the page and carried on.

*Today I began to tail the woman with the blue handkerchief. I know she's hiding something, but I don't yet know what. In the albums I found in her flat, some photographs had been recently added; old photographs, but printed just a few weeks ago. You don't start reorganizing your family albums when your father is dying in hospital. Perhaps it's just that she's a rebel, someone who wants to make a show of defiance; out of spite, perhaps, or maybe just on impulse. At all events, there's certainly something bogus about the way she prays. She is the daughter of a scientist; the man she sits with in the hospital might even be Davide Zago. But what I saw in her flat is not the library of a professor of philosophy. Yesterday I went to the land registry office. Everything seemed in order: the flat is registered in the name of Chiara Bonardi. I think she knows that I am not a pilgrim priest. But I want to see where it's all leading; what she is hiding behind that rosary she rattles off so confidently. If she is the atheist I think she is, I shall enjoy destroying her faith in man.*

Salazar closed his diary, took his pipe out of his suitcase and smoked the last bit of Afghan black. He had forgotten that it might be difficult to find in Rome.

During the night he woke up with a start, thinking he had heard someone outside the door. He looked at his watch: it was three o'clock, not the kind of time when nuns are on the move. He had left the shutters open, and the door leading into the corridor was white with moonlight. He listened hard: there was certainly movement of some sort. The shuffle of footsteps broke the silence once again. He heard a thud, and a window opening with a grating sound beyond the left-hand wall. That in itself was odd: none of the rooms near his own were occupied, except by linen and provisions of various kinds. He turned the key in the lock and went into the corridor, pistol cocked. One of the doors was open. He pressed back against the door-post, then bounded into the room. The windows were wide open, and the curtain cord was swaying gently, banging against the wall. He leant out over the windowsill and saw a shadow going down from the gallery into the courtyard. He heard yet more footsteps on the stone floor of the entrance hall, then the rasping of the gate as it was pulled shut. The following morning the sisters called the police. Thieves had made their way into the convent during the night and stolen some paintings from the refectory, but there were no signs of a forced break-in. Salazar looked suspiciously at the strips of roughly cut canvas dangling from the empty frames.

# II

He had looked for an internet point where he would not attract attention, and noted the cine cameras as he went in. There was an email message from Guntur, with an address near San Basilio. Now Salazar got out of the train and started walking along the dismal streets. He found the block of flats, which was on a corner, separated from the street by a double row of rubbish bins. Torn, faded hangings fluttered from the balconies, and the few plant pots contained nothing but weeds; old tyres, rusty fridges, bicycles and other household goods were propped up against the railings, several of which had been torn out; the stakes of the nearby fencing were all twisted. The concrete of the pavement had been smashed into so much gravel; in front of the garages, the comings and going of the cars had worn it away entirely, leaving a sea of mud. Salazar went up the poorly-lit stairway, found the landing of flat 117 and knocked, as he had been instructed, though not before unbuttoning his jacket and ensuring his pistol was at the ready. He heard steps, sensed that he was being spied on through the peep hole. Then the key turned in the lock, and a squat, bearded man who could have been South American appeared on the threshold. He looked around him and gestured to Salazar to go in, then quickly kicked the door shut behind him. Salazar took a few steps across the grubby floor, smelled the bitter scent of cooked resin and knew that he had come to the right place. At the end of the corridor he glimpsed a room, lit by electric light, where several men were busying themselves around some gas rings. The man was barring his way. He took a foil-wrapped packet out of his pocket and held it out to Salazar, then put his hands on his hips, giving them a shake every now and again, as though they were wet. He lifted them to touch his nose, then lowered them again, like a boxer before delivering a blow. Salazar lifted up a bit of foil, fingered the resin and sniffed his finger; from the scent, it seemed to be good quality Dutch. He wondered how on earth it had made its way to this God-forsaken spot. He nodded, and handed the Indian a roll of banknotes he had counted out in advance. The man leafed through them with expert fingers and tucked them away inside his shirt. His hands still going like a pair of dumb-bells, he whacked the lock, opened the door and thrust the inspector unceremoniously out of it.

In Zurich, in March, there may still be snow on the ground, lying along the edges of the streets, blackened by exhaust fumes, or in patches of shade in meadows, quite unlike the dazzling, fluffy snow on the peaks behind the town, which is a balm for eyes wearied by the glass and iron of the cityscape. You have to go through the dark brown of the countryside and the dull sheet metal of the goods sheds along the motorway to get to it. In the evening it becomes tinged with pink, whipped up into plumes by gusts of wind and driven against the rocks, on which it falls in a fine dust. On just such an evening, at the crossroads between Seilergraben and Muhlergasse, a Mercedes roared off while the lights were still red and knocked down a man on a pedestrian crossing. The traffic drew to a halt, horns sounded, people got out of their cars to see if they could help the victim, but it was too late. Anyone witnessing the scene from the Zelenka Versichherung building would have seen the Mercedes driving at full tilt towards the station and then taking the Bahnhofbrucke. The dead man was a forty-two year old Italian, the representative, in Switzerland, of a famous Milanese car firm. He was found to have been carrying a Glock 19, fitted with a silencer. The police started looking for witnesses on what was clearly a murder hunt. Someone had been quick enough to take down the details of the Mercedes' number plate, which turned out to have been stolen. It was found several days later in a parking lot just near the German border, with bloodstains on the front seat.

It was still early. The sun was beginning to warm up the damp air. Over the space of a few days, suburban lawns had turned a healthy shade of green, whose colour softened the grimness of the eastern outskirts. The puddles along the railway line reflected bright gashes of sky. The city, and the day, were emerging from the smoky darkness and suddenly seemed born anew. Even the graffiti-daubed carriages conveyed a sense of joy on that radiant morning. Salazar allowed himself to be rocked by the movement of the strangely empty train. He got out at the station for Saint Peter's and walked to the basilica. It was two days before Easter, and the canonization of Benedict XVI. The piazza had been cordoned off, and frenzied work was going ahead on erecting the podium from which the pope would greet the crowd after High Mass. A crane was hoisting the pieces of a giant crucifix on to a tubular construction which had been put up in front of the obelisk. Men in black were walking hurriedly up and down, talking quietly into minute microphones they wore around their necks; then they would place two fingers on the earphone, and slip it back inside their shirts. They would look up and signal to one another, unnoticed by the crowd amidst the other guards who were taking up their positions beneath the colonnade. A group of pilgrim friars from some Asian country were walking towards the square, led by a guide waving a yellow umbrella; they wore the grey habit of the missionary and the badge of the novice, and were careful to keep close to one another, their faces expressing reverence and awe. Endless rows of camper-vans were parked to either side of Via della Conciliazione, their roofs bristling with satellite aerials. Journalists and technicians were camping out en masse. The street was awash with cables, and the pavements were piled high with rolls of barbed wire which was to block access to the square. There was the sound of the odd trumpet. At the foot of the flight of steps, a squad of Swiss Guards, besieged by tourists clutching cameras, had gathered for a rehearsal of the forthcoming parade. Seeing their uniforms and halberds glistening in the sunlight, Salazar remembered the day he had sworn his oath. There had been the same light in the piazza, the same pink colour on the façade of the basilica. It had rained during the night, and the paving was still gleaming and clean-smelling. The procession of officers had come marching out of the Porta Angelica and lined up in four rows below the platform to the sound of a drum roll. The inspector had been beside himself with emotion, looking towards the throng of other people's relatives behind the barriers with tears in his eyes. He himself had no one to wave to, no one to walk with through the streets of Rome after the ceremony, proudly clad in his dress uniform. When he thought of his parents, he would remember those of his fellow students, glimpsed in framed photographs on bedside-tables in the dormitory, photographs he himself had never had

the opportunity of taking. He thought of the rubble in Haiti,
the sirens sounding, people wailing, bloodied and white with
dust. At such moments he would stare skywards and wonder
why things had to be as they were. The new prior had come
from Bologna for the ceremony. Salazar scarcely knew him,
he had left the patriarchal monastery before the new prior had
arrived. But he was pleased to be greeted by his old teachers,
and the odd companion who had remained in the city garrison.
Going into the basilica with them to hear mass, he felt that that
church was his home, and that everyone there recognized him
and greeted him, Domingo Salazar, the Haitian orphan who
had become an officer in the papal guard. Suddenly he felt that
the hard times were over, and that the rest of his life would be
one glorious march. He would continue to make his leaders
proud of him, and serve in the great army of the Church as it
progressed from victory to victory. His first enquiries, into the
kidnapping of the president of the Bishops' Conference which
his division had succeeded in foiling, gave him enormous
satisfaction. Cardinal Antonelli had been targeted by an anti-
papist group because of his reforms to the school syllabus. The
new law forbade the teaching of Darwinism, and introduced
creationism into the curriculum for the first time. Together
with blasphemy, thanks to Antonelli's law Darwinism too had
become a crime. Anyone advocating the ideas of the fanatical
Englishman might be hauled up before the courts. The first
negative verdicts were not long in coming, and many secular-
minded teachers left the profession. The terrorists belonging to
the group known as 'God is dead', who had been threatening
Antonelli for some time, had at last managed to get him in
their sights. The attack was to take place in the morning, when
as always he left for the ministry after mass in the Church
of San Francesco a Ripa. One group would be waiting for

him with a bogus ambulance, while others would block the access roads. The terrorists were planning a kidnap which would mortify the curia. But the papal police had infiltrated the group and managed to intercept their communications. The morning of the kidnap, the area was bristling with plainclothes-policemen, Salazar among them, and it was his company which surrounded the terrorists. The man who came out of the church wearing a cardinal's robes was not Antonelli, but a policeman; the real cardinal had stayed behind in safety in the sacristy. When the ambulance moved off in the prelate's direction, it was immediately attacked and boarded by the papal police, who immobilized the bogus nurses. The anti-papist network was completely broken up and the whole of the fourth police district was awarded a medal for valour. Salazar's commanding officer took a shine to his new recruit and commended him to the secret services. Over the years that followed, Salazar had specialized in Catholic propaganda and was sent abroad, first to Beirut, then to Amsterdam, his second posting, where his cover was that he was mustering the Dutch Catholics. His real work, however, lay elsewhere: he was to sabotage the secular state, spread distrust in science, intercept the anti-papist refugees from Italy and keep them under surveillance. A flock of pigeons, swooping down on some maize scattered at the friars' feet, distracted him from his thoughts. For a moment, Salazar had felt an upsurge of the enthusiasm of those early years. What had changed in the meantime? He now thought back to his youthful naiveté with some surprise; and yet, protected by such innocence, he had been happy. Now his main emotion was one of bitterness at no longer knowing what was right. He was a warrior in the service of the Church, but he was surrounded by incompetence, indifference and pettiness, by men who sought only their own personal advantage.

Perhaps, indeed, it was just a matter of age. He thought of the vicar, and wondered if he were beginning to resemble him: was he too becoming a dinosaur, self-important, lacking all sensitivity and intuition? If so, that was a tendency that had to be fought against at all costs: he must never lose sight of the supreme aim of all he did, namely the triumph of faith. He had to remain a hound of God, a steadfast warrior in his chosen war; he owed this to the Church which had saved him, to the men who had given him his faith. Picking his way among the pigeons, he went into a bar, bought two metro tickets and went off towards Ponte Vittorio Emanuele. Once back in his room, he drew the shutters closed against the sun, already high in the sky, turned the key in the lock and smoked a whole pipeful of what was indeed an excellent Nether Dope.

Ivan Zago had now been on the run for a week. Wherever he went, he felt that he was followed. It could not go on like this. By now he had wandered all over Germany. It was not money that was the problem; he had plenty of that. His job as a doctor travelling the world for various oil companies had netted him a decent nest egg. But whenever he went back to Zurich between engagements, the curia's cut-throats were instantly on his tail. The last one – a greenhorn who was at least one step behind him – had had to be blown away. He hadn't realized that Ivan had spotted him. On the evening when the papal agent had left his lair to come out to kill him, Ivan had waited for him outside the hotel and shot him down with a stolen gun. Now he could no longer go back to Zurich. It was too risky; his next engagement was not until July, on an offshore oil well in Alaska. He thought all this would have come to an end with his father's death. When he had learned that his father was seriously ill in hospital, Ivan had stopped blackmailing them, hoping that they would then leave his father in peace, that they wouldn't persist in hounding a dying man. But in fact they had taken him hostage; they thought that Ivan would concede defeat and give himself up. Indeed, in a sudden fit of rage, he had been about to do so; he was ready to sacrifice himself to save his father further suffering. Then his father had died, alone and left to his own devices in a hospital for infectious diseases. Ivan certainly had no intention of calling it a day; he would make them pay for it, and he wanted his revenge to be carefully considered. But the curia wasn't calling it a day either; by now Novak must have been running scared. All the better! The problem had to be solved at its source: he would have to go to Rome and settle his score with Novak. That same night, after almost two years, he phoned Marta.

Things seemed unusually busy when he arrived at the hospital. The sisters' office was closed and the police were denying access to relatives who had come for the evening visit. Salazar went into the corridor with the light brown linoleum and saw a group of nurses clustered around the bed of patient 148.

'What's going on?' he asked the doctor with the goatee, who was coming out of the room.

'There's been a death. But there don't seem to be any suspicious circumstances.'

'Bonardi?'

'Yes. Cardiac arrest. We're just taking the readings.'

'When did it happen?'

'Last night. Well, shortly before dawn, according to the police doctor.'

'Have the relatives been informed? Does his daughter know?'

'We phoned her, but there was no answer. Her mobile was

switched off. She's probably on her way now – it's visiting time. We'll soon be letting the relatives in.'

Salazar drew the man to one side and spoke to him quietly.

'Doctor... you realize that I shall have to see the body?'

'Don't worry. I've already given orders to that effect. You can come in now. The other patient has been moved.' With those words, the doctor nodded to the nurses who were standing in the doorway. Then he turned to Salazar and rapped him lightly on the chest with his knuckles, smiling as he did so.

'I told you, inspector, you should have looked for this man's guardian angel. Perhaps he's still around! A wingless angel never wanders far. Basically they are functionaries, just like ourselves. He'll be waiting to hear about his new job. Maternity is on the fourth floor!' he added with a sarcastic grin.

Salazar couldn't decide whether the man was joking or being completely serious. He hurried towards Bonardi's room.

The body had been moved on to a stretcher and two doctors were examining it. It was yellowish, almost leaden in colour, it no longer looked as if it were made of flesh; the rigid limbs, and the hands, in plastic gloves, had adopted grotesque positions. The face was ashen, the mouth freed at last from the anguished grimace into which pain had forced it for so long. Now it seemed impossible that that tangle of bones might once have been alive. With practised movements, without exchanging a word, the two doctors examined the body. The nurse was leaning up against the bedside table, filling in various documents; she waited until the photographic readings had been completed, then covered up what remained of the engineer Marco Bonardi with a white cloth.

'Nothing untoward. No signs of violence,' said the police doctor to Salazar, lowering his mask. But then he added:

'Just two small marks under the left armpit; like two burns. We don't know what they are. You see?' He lifted the cloth and raised the dead man's arm to show Salazar two little black marks the width of the head of a nail.

'But they might be bedsores, or lesions the patient himself caused; for example, indentations made by two pyjama buttons, pressed against his skin by the weight of his own body.'

The doctor pulled the cloth up again, and two stretcher-bearers wheeled the body from the room. Salazar began to study one of them carefully: he had a hooked nose and a wrinkled neck, his shoulders were slightly hunched, and he had a swaying walk. Salazar listened to the way he spoke, noted the way he moved; he thought he recognized him as one of the two men he'd caught by surprise in the prayer room. Then he turned his attention to the other man, who was now signing the papers which the nurse handed him. He could not be certain they were the same men; it had been too dark for him to see their faces; he had seen them only in profile. Nonetheless, he memorized the names on their identification badges; he would see whether there was anything suspicious in their CVs later, when he got their files from the vicar.

'We'll look into matters more thoroughly after the family has been notified of the death. For the moment we cannot touch the body,' said the police doctor, following the nurse and his colleague into the corridor. Meanwhile the sister had opened the gate and the relatives had filed into the unit. Salazar felt a sudden premonition. He stayed on for a time in room 148, which was now empty, then scanned the small crowd in the entrance hall and went down the stairs to the vending machine. There was no one there. It was then that he realized that the dead man was not Marco Bonardi, but Davide Zago. And whoever the woman in the blue handkerchief was, she had achieved her aim.

Since escaping from the re-education centre almost ten years ago, after having been sentenced for having had an abortion, Marta Quinz had been in hiding. She had been given a five-year sentence for having aborted the child she had conceived as a result of a rape. She had just started working as a doctor in the maternity department of a Milanese hospital when she was struck by a tragedy which was to change her life. Two guardians of the faith were on her trail because they suspected her of allowing newborn babies with serious impairments to die, but they could not come up with any conclusive evidence against her, and this enraged them. They had lain in wait for her one night in the hospital parking lot and bundled her into a car; they had threatened and beaten her, telling her that she would have to confess if she didn't want something worse to happen. Marta had held out against their blows; if she had talked, dozens of families would have been incriminated, dozens of mothers would have ended up in prison. Her kidnappers were convinced that she would blurt out the truth at the first slap; they had not expected such resistance. The car had stopped at a traffic light, and Marta had managed to jump out, but they had managed to catch up with her and had given her a hard night. They had not even bothered to cover their faces, so certain were they that they would get off scot-free. They had left her bleeding on a street on the outskirts of town, and had she not received help from a tramp who was sleeping rough under a bridge over the motorway, she would have died. She did not want to report a rape: if a woman became pregnant as a result, she was obliged to carry the pregnancy to term.

Marta had asked for help from a colleague in the hospital. In the distant past, she and Ivan had had an affair, a long-standing relationship which had somehow recently petered out; through apathy, perhaps, she was not really sure.

Ivan had taken care of everything. He had bribed a male nurse to leave him the keys of an operating theatre, and one January night he had performed an abortion on Marta in the very department where she worked. They had left the clinic together, in a car belonging to the medical police, using a forged pass supposedly belonging to one of its members. But someone had informed on them, and the guardians of the faith had obliged Marta to undergo a medical examination. The result left no room for doubt. They were both found guilty of illegal abortion; he had been sentenced to ten years in prison, while she had managed to escape, had gone into hiding, and was now in charge of the Roman branch of the Free Death Brigades, her photograph still on the wanted persons list. But time, and a certain amount of ingenuity, had helped her to become less recognizable; she knew better than anyone else who her enemies were, and had learned the art of self-disguise accordingly. She had narrowly avoided arrest on two occasions, when she had helped other women who were seeking abortions. The police had ransacked her illicit clinic, breaking in just before she received a warning. But then the Free Death Brigade had changed tack. It was less risky to help women to go abroad for their abortions; a holiday in Corsica or the Balearic Islands would serve as cover. But the police were becoming aware of what was going on, and were now asking for ultrasound scans for certain destinations. During those same days the Roman branch was planning a deadly coup: an attempt on the pope's life in Saint Peter's Square on the day

of Benedict XVI's canonization would have caused the whole
world to quake. Marta and her associates had been waiting
for such an opportunity for years. Preparations for the coup
had exposed them to considerable risk. The members of the
Free Death Brigade financed themselves through kidnapping
and pushing drugs. Many of them had been arrested; the group
had been virtually decimated. Marta was almost at breaking
point, but she couldn't give up now. Sometimes she regretted
that she couldn't lead a normal life, with a husband, a job and
children to bring up. It hadn't worked out with Ivan; yet while
they were together, he had seemed to be the love of her life.
She fell in love with him immediately, gave herself over to
an all-engulfing passion, which suddenly gave meaning to her
life and even had the power to deaden the all-consuming rage
within her. The more helpless she felt in its sudden grip, the
more serenely she yielded to it. He on the other hand had never
managed to fall in love with her. He swore that he loved her,
and in a sense it was true; but Ivan was a highly educated man,
he used his head rather than his heart, and went about things
with a doggedness which robbed his actions of spontaneity.
Marta felt as though she were his daughter, rather than his
lover; it was as though he were waiting for her to grow up
so that he could let her go. Their being together had turned
into an absurd expectation of her future maturity. They built
nothing together, they were not even a real couple; he talked
a great deal about the idea of the family, but the minute they
were alone together all the life went out of him, he seemed
to go into a decline; he seemed sad. He assured her that this
wasn't so, it was just that he was slow and careful by nature;
but Marta could see that sadness was precisely what it was; or
perhaps rather a repressed boredom, which was even worse.
Ivan tried to convince himself that being with Marta was doing

him good, but his whole nature was nudging him elsewhere. He had always scorched everything around him; he was made to be alone. So now Marta had nobody. Her father and mother were long dead, and she had no other family. This helped her to bear the weight of a life lived out in hiding. Hiding was not a problem, indeed she was quite happy to stay hidden; it spared her the need for choice. She was not vulnerable, there was no one in the outside world whom the police could pursue in order to track her down. At times, when she was sitting with those whom she helped to die, she felt that it was they who were her family: that army of dying people who looked at her with gratitude even as their faces were contorted with pain.

The door was opened by an old woman with unkempt white hair and thick glasses. She stood in front of him without saying a word, her trembling hands pressed to her chest. Perhaps she had been expecting him. Her eyes were red; clearly, she had been crying, and her mouth was half-open, set, as though she were trying to repress further tears. She was wearing an apron over a grey wool dress, and shapeless carpet slippers; one of her stockings had slipped down almost to her ankle. Salazar went into the flat, leaving her at the door. The room at the end of the corridor, where Chiara slept, was now empty. The bed was made up in the double bedroom, though there was only one pillow. The lamps had been plugged in, and the wardrobe was now full of female garments, on coat hangers; old woman's clothes, long and dark. The Panama hat was still there, on a shelf, together with the odd towel. A large half-open suitcase stood in one corner. Salazar realized that this was the home of an elderly widow. Now at last everything made sense. He noticed things that had escaped his attention on his first visit: the yellowing curtains, the knitted bedcover made with scraps of leftover wool, the piles of old newspapers, a rickety table, a peeling mirror in a bamboo frame. He went quickly into the living room and opened the photograph albums. The more recent photos had been removed, but oddly enough their absence left no gaps: if looked at in sequence, these images told another story entirely. All traces of Chiara had vanished. The photos were of other children, nephews and nieces or friends of the lonely couple who had spent their lives going from one oil well to another. Chiara had replaced the old woman for just as long as it took her to bring about her husband's death. She had pretended to be his daughter, and a devout Catholic, so as to be allowed into the palliative care unit. She had gone to live in the Bonardi's flat and had the old woman hidden elsewhere; she must belong to a well-organized network if she could afford to arrange such things. Had Chiara herself gone into the hospital during the night, when the unit was under surveillance, or had the job been done by her fellow-conspirators? In that way, Bonardi's death would not have aroused suspicion. But how had he died? What poison, what weapon were used by the angels of death? Salazar went back into the hallway. The old woman had shuffled quietly after him from room to room; now she was looking at him apprehensively from the kitchen doorway. A pan was boiling on the stove, causing the windows to mist over. The battered formica table was set with a soup plate, a spoon, a glass and a napkin. Salazar could smell the broth. Now he turned and looked at the old woman who was leaning up against the door frame, clearly rigid with fear. With a sudden shudder, he sensed that this house, though full of pain, had been freed of some ghostly presence. He went off without a word. When the automatic light on the stairs went out, a trembling hand on the fourth floor switched it on again.

The hairdresser's and the beauty salon were barely thirty metres apart. Salazar went in and approached the first assistant who came to hand.

'Excuse me, may I ask you a few questions?' he said, pointing to his badge. The girl was mixing a dye. Before she could reply, a heavily made-up woman intervened.

'Can I help you?' she asked, edging Salazar towards the door. She was chewing gum, and smelled strongly of violets.

'I'm looking for this woman,' said Salazar, taking the photo of Chiara Bonardi out of his pocket and edging the woman backwards in his turn.

'Do you know her? She came to your establishment on 27 February.' The woman took the photograph and put on the glasses which had been hanging round her neck; she looked at the face for a moment, frowning.

'That's Signora Loiacano! How young she looks! Look, Teresa!' Salazar snatched the photograph from her hand.

'Do you know where she lives? Does she come here often?'

'She's been a client of ours for years. But I don't know where she lives. I think she's local, though, because I often see her go by with shopping bags.'

'Thank you,' said Salazar, and slipped out of the shop under the curious gaze of the two assistants. He wandered aimlessly through the streets around Piazza Risorgimento, looking at people at the tram stops, in shop windows and doorways with the secret hope of catching the woman by surprise. She lived round here; at this very moment she might be in the supermarket on the corner or the café opposite, or perhaps, unknown to him, she was at some window, observing him from behind the curtains. Salazar looked up at the uncommunicative façades of the buildings which lined the street: closed curtains, blinds half-down, the frosted glass of surgeries and offices.

Diego Marani

He looked at his watch: by now it was two o'clock and he hadn't had anything to eat. He went into a bar and ordered a sandwich, casting an eye at the television that was hanging from the wall, at the piles of Easter eggs in the window and at the headlines of the newspaper being read by the man seated at the bar's only table. The man had heavy, stumpy hands; when he put down the paper, Salazar saw that it was the South American from San Basilio!

*I've missed a trick here, no two ways about it. I should have followed the woman throughout the day, and searched the flat on Via Cornelia from top to bottom. I made a play at catching her out; in fact, the opposite has happened. I didn't think that things in Italy had come to such a pass. These Free Death Brigades mean business. I am far from convinced that self-serving orthodoxy is the most effective strategy. Ever since abortion, the pill, assisted fertilization and euthanasia were proclaimed terrorist offences, anonymous accusations have been raining down on the desks of the papal police, and those in charge of anti-terrorist activities have been wasting their time hunting down a handful of offenders in order to be able to boast of some headline-grabbing arrest. University professors, journalists, even the odd priest have fallen into the trap. Banner headlines, triumphal announcements, everyone congratulating everyone else, but where does this get us? Here every member of the hierarchy dons the mantle of defender of the faith and vies with all others in observance of the Catholic rule - purely to earn promotion, to curry favour, to procure themselves important positions in the curia. But, by so doing, such men lose sight of their goal. Here we see that same obtuseness which caused us such bitter setbacks in the past. Dogma is to be used against atheists, not against ourselves.*

*There is no point in even trying to cure incurable ills. Giving placebos instead of drugs would solve the problem of euthanasia, as well as exposing the limits of what medicine can do. Courts sitting in judgement on the course of a disease serve no purpose, indeed they are counterproductive. The principle is correct: a sick person cannot take his own life because it is not his to take, it has been bestowed on him by God. But when decisions about treatment are entrusted to a court, and not to the patient himself, or to his family, then inevitably there will be ill-feeling. There are other, less controversial ways of taking this decision out of his hands. Indeed, he should be allowed to choose his own treatment: he will never know what is in the pills that he swallows. What counts, all in all, is not to prolong a man's life for as long as possible, but to remind him that death is his destiny. That way, he is more likely to give himself over to the Church. What the curia is interested in above all is getting its hands on the property of the euthanasiasts, and it may thus be seen as gaining material advantage from the situation; but that is tantamount to paving the way for the angels of death. I shall draw attention to this paradox in my report on this mission. Perhaps some enlightened spirit in the curia will read it.*

*I'm worried about Guntur; he hasn't answered my last emails. It's too risky to telephone him. I'll try and contact him again by email tomorrow at the same time. There's an internet point near the church of Sant'Andrea della Valle.*

That Friday, the church seemed to be empty. The canon who normally stayed behind to tidy up the missals had already left; no one had come to clean the candlesticks or empty the collection boxes. Then Salazar saw the curtain being pulled back and caught sight of the black shoes, but when he knelt down in the confessional he was surprised not to smell the usual scent of mouthwash. Obeying orders, he recited the Credo, gave his registration number and launched into his speech.

'Vicar, I have news. A man died in the hospital. At first sight it looked like a natural death, but I'm sure it was euthanasia. Unfortunately the angel of death slipped through my fingers, but now I'm on the scent. I may even have a name. I know how they operate…'

Hearing unusual sounds from behind the grille, Salazar broke off. He noticed that the curtain on the other side was half-drawn. He glimpsed something glittering, then heard the click of a gun being loaded. He threw himself out of the confessional just as three bullets fired from a pistol with a silencer hissed through the brass grating and sank into the marquetry, splintering carved *putti* and garlands as they did so. Staggering around behind a pillar, Salazar managed to pull out his own gun, fired several shots in the direction of the confessional, then rushed to take refuge behind the chapel wall. The shots reverberated through the church like thunder; a light rain of shattered plaster pattered down on to the floor. Huddled on the ground, the inspector strained his ears, expecting further shots. For one brief moment the distant din of the traffic could be heard through the silence. Then a thud, the crash of overturned chairs and, a few moments later, a sound of shuffling coming from the high altar. Salazar trained his gun on the shadowy figure which had appeared on the stairs below. The canon, who had come back into the church on hearing the sound of the fracas, was holding up his hands and shaking his head; rigid with fear, he was staring into space, his chin quivering. Then Salazar emerged from behind his pillar and ran into the nave, peering between the rows of benches towards the confessional. Stretched out in a puddle of blood lay a man half-enveloped in the purple curtain which he had brought down with him as he fell, his gun still in his hand. Salazar went closer and turned the body over. He was a young man, with an olive complexion and a haircut like that of a cadet; his eyes were wide open – both of them. Salazar went through his pockets, extracting a bunch of keys, a mobile phone, two cartridge clips and a badge just like his own. The man was a Dominican.

A north wind had got up, giving a sheen to the paving and the façades of the houses, whipping up swirls of dust which settled on car bonnets. An empty tram jangled along Corso Vittorio Emanuele; the last shutters were coming down. Salazar walked fast, avoiding passers-by, trying to collect his thoughts. The person who had killed the vicar clearly knew about their meetings; perhaps he had been on his trail ever since his arrival in Rome. That would explain the unexpected visitors to the convent. It would also solve the mystery of the stolen paintings. It was him they were looking for. He had not expected such reckless behaviour; he had been proved wrong. These people are dangerous, he thought; but now they were the only trail he had. Someone was undoubtedly lying in wait for him in the convent. That was where he had to go. He was well aware that it was dangerous; but he had to amass further proof. He went into the first church he came upon, to get his breath back and consider his situation. The silence and the scent of incense calmed him. He took his aggressor's mobile phone out of his pocket. The address book had just ten numbers, referred to by the signs of the zodiac, but he did not have the password. He thought of the dead man, the supposed cadet, who had probably just left the academy; he imagined the lectures his superiors would have given him. Suddenly sure of himself, he typed in *domini canis*, and found just one file, headed *Semana Santa*. It was a plan of the security measures for Benedict XVI's canonization ceremony, down to the last detail: the make-up of the squads of guards, the positions of the marksmen and telecameras, the route to be taken by the pope, the seating arrangements for the great and the good on the podium, the teams who would be manning the police vehicles, the general running-order, with comments, and the timing of the entry of the various groups for the final parade. Salazar read it carefully. Useful though it was, he could not run the risk of keeping that phone in his possession. When he had memorized its contents as best he could, he took out the battery and removed the microchip, broke it in two and threw the pieces into the vases of cut flowers on the altar. Now he had to brace himself to return to the convent.

In Civitavecchia Harbour three men were waiting nervously in the embarkation parking lot. Two of them were seated in a car, with the windows down. The third, a thin man with very fair hair, was pacing up and down in front of the bonnet, smoking a cigarette. Then he propped his elbows up on one of the open windows.

'You and Boris stay in the car. I'll do the talking.' The others nodded. It was almost evening, and lights were going on along the quays. The ferry from Genoa was drawing alongside: all lit up, it set the water foaming, its funnels sending out clouds of black smoke. The cars began rattling down the gangway, and soon a long queue had formed at the exit from the parking lot. The fair-haired man threw down his butt end and got into the driving seat. A group of harbour-workers in blue overalls set off towards the bar, taking off their caps and wiping the sweat from their foreheads. One of them, who had stayed behind, went up to the car and said in a low voice:

'That's the one, that yellow TIR that's coming down right now.'

The fair-haired man switched on the engine and looked towards the yellow truck that was bumping down the gangway. He turned the car round on the quay, tyres screeching, and joined the queue of cars leaving the harbour. The truck slithered after him. They made their way slowly forward, one behind the other, as far as the service area outside Santa Severa, where the truck driver parked in the small empty square and went to check the tarpaulins. He was middle-aged, fresh-complexioned, solidly-built, and slow-moving; his head was shaven, but his chin bore the faint suggestion of a beard. He had a ring in his left ear, a snake tattooed on his upper arm, and he was wearing shorts and flashy trainers. The fair-haired man stopped the car some distance away from him, just beyond the turn-off to the petrol station. He gave the others a tense nod, pulled something out from under the seat and walked off towards the truck, then addressed the man behind the trailer.

'Good evening, I'm Sergio's contact.'

The driver pretended not to hear; he just stood there, tightening a strap. The fair-haired man went a bit closer.

'Semtex. Altogether, a kilo in all. Plus the detonators. We've agreed on a price,' he said, lowering his voice. The driver nodded. The fair-haired man took a folded newspaper out from under his shirt.

'To be handed over in two instalments. Next one, same place, same time.'

The driver nodded, stuffed the newspaper into his trouser pocket, winked, went off towards the driver's cab and started the engine; the truck moved slowly off, suddenly lit up from nose to tail with coloured lights. The sky over the dark sea, still red from the sunset, was casting a golden glow over the houses in the little bay. The fair-haired man was just about to go back to the car when he heard shouting. Two four-by-fours with darkened windows were now blocking the car's exit, one in front and one behind. Armed men were surrounding it, ordering the other two to get out and put up their hands. The fair-haired man squatted down among the bushes in the flower-bed and proceeded on all fours towards the wall of the motorway restaurant. The truck slithered slowly down the road leading to the petrol station on the other side of the little square, and there the fair-haired man climbed into it through the open window. At that moment two police cars drove into the service area, sirens blaring. Scarlet in the face, the driver first tried to push the man out again, then pulled him up on to the seat and gestured to him to hide on the bunk bed, swearing in his own language as he did so. He drove the truck towards the motorway, gradually picking up speed, peering nervously into the rear-view mirror and gesticulating furiously at the cars which were overtaking him, hooting wildly.

He held his breath, hoping that that would enable him to hear better. The time switch was ticking away in the entrance hall, and that ticking sound was a time bomb. Salazar looked for the button with the orange pilot light so that he could press it when the moment came. The further along the corridor he went, the colder the air became. There was no longer the usual smell of vinegar, no candle lit before the statue of the Virgin. The glass doors were open. Salazar slipped through the first one, gun levelled. The first room was empty, as was the next, and the last one was occupied only by bags of linen, heaped up on the floor. Salazar went up the stairs three steps at a time, flattening himself against the wall. When he reached the first floor, he raised his pistol and slipped behind the pillar supporting the stairs. Then the light went out; a hinge creaked and Salazar fired, three shots into the warm belly of the darkness. He stood stock-still. But he sensed movement: someone, apart from himself, was breathing. The switch for the automatic light was too far away, on the other side of the stairs; to reach it, he would have had to cross the area lit up by the skylight. He inched forwards along the wall; he heard a scuffling sound, a thud and then the din of a volley of bullets, shattering the plaster on the wall behind him. He fired another random shot, then threw himself to the ground. When silence fell again, he heard the sizzling of an electric cable, giving out sparks, and the sound of plaster flaking down on to the benches. He got up and dusted himself down; now the switch was right in front of him, just by the half-open door of his room, but it had been pulled out of the wall. He was about to jump to the other side of the stairs when he stumbled and fell against the soft mass of a lifeless body, pushing the door of his room fully open as he did so. At that same moment, a sign flashed on outside the skylight, casting a mauve gleam over the face of a bald man who was lying on his back on the floor in a pool of blood, his sub-machinegun protruding from beneath his blood-spattered ribs, his arms and legs spread-eagled and his fingers weirdly splayed. He was young and solidly built, and his still open mouth suggested surprise. Salazar went through his pockets, which yielded some scraps of paper, a wad of banknotes, a key and a railway ticket for Milan, with a reserved seat for Saturday March 11. Salazar got to his feet: he had to get out of there, and fast. He had a quick look into his room: the cupboard was open, and empty, the camp-bed stripped; all his possessions had disappeared.

Salazar went off through the flickering lamplight, peering over his shoulder as he did so, trying to collect his thoughts. He had now lost contact with his superiors; in order to get back in touch, he would have to put himself in the hands of the Swiss Guards, and that was a tricky business. They were always extremely thorough: they would detain him, then interrogate him and check his fingerprints. It would be a few days before he could continue his enquiries. The Piazza Karol Wojtyla Barracks were the nearest, but perhaps it would be better to go straight to the Porta Angelica. He stopped at a fountain in a small square to wash off the blood from his clothes and hands. Perhaps he should not have left the convent in such a hurry; perhaps he should have looked around more thoroughly. Where had the nuns gone? Had they been locked away somewhere? Kidnapped, even? At all events, the whole thing had been badly managed; there was no need for such high-octane action, such hullabaloo. He could have been caught and done away with much more discreetly. Thinking back to the empty rooms, it struck him that the place must have been suddenly evacuated. Then he saw why: it wasn't a convent at all! He remembered that he had never seen more than three nuns at any one time, had never heard any noise, smelled any cooking. The place was too empty to have been really lived in. So, it had been nothing more than a stage-set. Why had it taken so long for the penny to drop? But then nothing made sense any more. Who was the man in the confessional? Who had set that trap for him? Salazar moved off from the fountain, horror-struck. So the vicar was a spy? He ran off, taking the darkest alley he could find.

He watched them as they met up, emerging from porches and alleyways. There were four of them; at first he thought they were just passers-by, people coming out to smoke a cigarette. One had a dog on a lead; another was taking a lighter out of his pocket. Salazar began to run, but the four men behind him were on his trail. Incredible though it seemed, at that hour the streets around Campo Marzio were all empty. Coming to a place where the street widened out, he tried to hide behind some parked cars, but his pursuers were on his trail. They dragged him out and stood him up in front of a street door, opened up their jackets and brought out their guns. Salazar lifted his hands slowly above his head and let himself be disarmed. He tried to look them in the eye, to memorize their faces; before he could do so, he felt a sharp stab of pain in the nape of his neck and lost consciousness.

He felt a macabre relish in slipping it into his mouth before placing it in his eye socket. That slippery sphere gave him a dizzy sense of power. He could eat the eye he had not got. He imagined himself swallowing his organ of sight and seeing inside himself, he who could not see outside himself. What effect would that have? He spat his prosthesis out into his hand, put it in the empty ashtray and took two little bottles out of a drawer. He sprinkled the lubricant on to the silicone eye and put it in, then washed out his mouth with the strawberry-scented mouthwash. Now he was whole again. He put the bottles back into the drawer and opened the envelope on the table. He took a black exercise-book out of it and started to read Salazar's diary, which his agents had just brought to him from Amsterdam.

## 24 April

*First I should say how I met Guntur, who he is, what he does.
But I'm in such a hurry to tell the story of Django that I don't
know where to start: thoughts are piling up in my head and
the words are getting all tangled up on the page. This whole
business is a bombshell, indeed it may even portend the death
of the Church as we know it. But it's better that no one in Rome
should hear about it; they would overreact, as usual, and only
make things worse. Until I've thought of some way out, I'll
keep it to myself. Guntur is older than me by some ten years,
but he seems very young; his face too is strangely youthful,
he's got no spare flesh on his frame, he is self-disciplined and
unassuming. His high cheekbones and narrow eyes add a touch
of mystery. He survived the tsunami which struck Indonesia in
2004 and, like me, he grew up in an orphanage, run by a Dutch
Muslim charitable body. He likes to say that only orphans can
be good Muslims, because the Prophet was an orphan too.
Normal people, who grow up in a family, don't know what it
means not to be able to call any woman mother, nor any man
father. Guntur is a neuro-psychiatrist, he is doing research at
the University of Amsterdam and in his spare time he helps out
in a madrassa in Slotervaart. We first met a couple of months
ago, and immediately clicked; we're both survivors, after all.
We both regard our existence as a joke played by providence,
and this helps us not to become attached to people, or to things,
and to realize that one day we will lose everything. Guntur is
a scientist, but he is also a sincere believer. His is the science
of Avicenna, that is, a science which proves the existence of
God and uses faith to cast light on reason. Guntur had agreed
to talk about the Gospels in the madrassa, and it was with*

*him that I organized the first Biblical-Koranist groups. I have set the missionary priests they send me from Rome to praying along with the imams; that way, they will be more useful than saying mass for a handful of senile old women in the Church of Sint Nicolaas. Let's hope that the people in Rome won't be too quick to notice what's going on. There is a lot at stake for me. I should have sought protection in the curia before embarking on such a risky venture. Anyway, it's too late now. Perhaps there is still someone in Bologna who knows me, some fellow student from the Patriarchal Monastery. I should make a visit sometime. But I'm so happy here. This year spring has been particularly lovely in Amsterdam, with the sky a constantly changing shade of blue, and the wind bringing a smell of earth, tearing the clouds into a thousand tatters the moment they form. The canals seem deeper, and below the surface another city teems with life, a city of fish on bicycles. In the evening it often rains, but it's like fine spray, light as a watering hose, prolonging the lives of the tulips and keeping the grass green. Guntur and I often meet up in a coffee shop on the Oudezijds. We talk about philosophy and faith, helped along by a pipeful of good Himalaya Cream.*

*28 April*

*This morning we woke up to thick mist, which is unusual at this time of year. I could tell it was misty because of the bicycle bells: when it's misty, they sound as though they're ringing underwater. The mist didn't rise until midday, but even then the sun didn't come out. And I had various irritating problems: that business with the money raised its head again. I had to go to the bank to explain. Rome sends me too much at a time, and I can't invest it all immediately; money laundering takes time. I can't start buying diamonds! I've tried to explain things to the Papal Nuncio, and he always promises that he'll talk it over with the Secretary of State. Meanwhile, I'm in danger of being accused of money laundering by the Dutch Customs Service. If they think I'm going to start going all over Europe with suitcases full of banknotes, they'll have to think again! They'll have to take on a mafioso to do that for them. I don't understand their strategy here either. If we must engage in money laundering, let's do it properly. With a good investment plan we'd run fewer risks and do better business. For example, how about them setting me up with a nice slush fund! It works like that here too. Why not pay some newspaper to write what we want, instead of insisting that we sell our own, which no one reads? Or why not invest in marine insurance, or armaments or container ships? That would mean sure-fire profit and less snooping. I keep on sending reports to Rome with details from firms which are up for sale, but I might as well not bother.*

*2 May*

*Today Guntur took me to his madrassa again. Some of the old men still mutter when they see the crucifix in my lapel, but they all hear me out, and when I read the psalms, some of them recite them with me. It is clear that we are all praying to the same God. Guntur pointed out that the Koran almost always speaks of believers, very rarely of Muslims, and in his view this is proof that Mohammed's first followers made no distinction between themselves and the Christians or Jews. They felt that they were all part of the one single faith; the real difference was with the others, the pagans and above all the atheists. The Slotervaart Muslims are well-organized. They have their own schools, which are better than those run by the state, their own social security system, their own doctors. They send their children to Arab universities, but then have them come back here. Holland is their country, and Muslims are in the majority in the cities; only the provinces are Protestant, though there are still a few Catholics in the south. The people in Rome would like me to spend time among them, to go to Maastricht to distribute catechisms in the schools; they fail to understand the game that is being played around these parts.*

*8 May*

*Sometimes I am puzzled by Guntur's attitude to science, and I think that even in his own world he is regarded as an oddity. For Muslims the only aim of science is to explain, to transmit, never to query or investigate. Guntur on the other hand has no qualms about discovering things which might put God's truth in doubt, indeed he maintains that one should never hesitate to follow the path along which doubt leads us. Yesterday evening in the Coffee Shop we had a disagreement. My view was that scientific discoveries are our own miracles: they are inexplicable, they can lead only to further wonderment. However far man may push himself, even in tinkering with life itself, the result will never be his own creation; at most, it will be mere rejigging. But Guntur disagreed.*

*'If God leads me to make discoveries which put my faith in doubt, it is because He wants to point me down another road to come to Him. Religion is like science. Without free and open debate, it withers and dies, leaving the road open to atheism. It is rational proof that thwarts attempts at undermining faith. The greatest discovery that science constantly presents us with is our own ignorance, and that is why the believer should have no fear of it. Today neither Christianity nor Islam can provide*

*answers to mankind's problems. Christ and Mohammed are but remote memories: it is so long since God sent us a sign. We are like a vessel wandering through space which has lost all contact with its base. If for thousands of years man has been getting no nearer to God, it must be because we have taken a wrong path. Science may help us find the right one.'*

*12 May*

*I sense that Guntur wants to tell me something, but he can't quite bring himself to do so. Perhaps he does not trust me, and this upsets me. Today he told me what he is working on at the university, namely, mirror neurons. Apparently he knew Neil Corrigan; he has read all his books. He cannot know that I was responsible for the suicide of his colleague at Imperial College. But Guntur is a scientist of another kind.*

*14 May*

*Guntur has gone to Zeeland for a few days, for a conference. He left only yesterday, but we have been emailing each other constantly: in the form of letters, which is what we like to do. I tell him about what I have been reading, about my various battle plans; he sends me little drawings of conference life, a sort of real time chronicle of his day, meetings with old windbags and a visit to the dyke on the Scheldt. I feel as if I am there with him. I didn't know about the old wool trade between Holland and Scotland which he mentions. I should really travel a bit more: I have been in Holland for years, but I have never been to Zeeland, nor to Friesland.*

*18 May*

*Today Guntur and I took the ferry to Enkhuizen and went for a trip on the Markermeer. It was a gloriously sunny day, the kind you don't often get in this part of the world. Along the coast we saw fields of tulips and old windmills, just like in a Dutch landscape! On the boat there were fishing rods for hire, and you could buy live bait. So we started to fish, without catching anything, of course. Even the little boys beside us were reeling in one herring after another, whereas all we did was to lose our bait. But Guntur seemed to enjoy it enormously, laughing amidst the spray, and smiling that disarming smile of his which makes everything seem like a small miracle. At times, when I'm alone, I too try to be amazed by little things, I try to wonder at the clouds, driven by the wind, at a flower closing its petals as evening approaches, at the fire burning in the fireplace. But I never succeed; all I do is to get bored. Clearly, I am not the meditative type!*

*On the beach at Enkhuizen we ate* poffertjes *in a bar that was raised on piles. Everything in it smelled of fried food, even the gardenias on the windowsills. For some reason, it was full of English, the kind who wear trainers and baseball caps; they walked as though they were drunk, dazed by too much sun. The dunes were covered with such rich, green vegetation that the effect was almost Mediterranean. At a certain point a group of horsemen came galloping across the beach. Guntur rushed up to them to have a closer look. He said he remembered horses from his early childhood, galloping along beaches just like this. Then his mood darkened.*

*'Have you ever been back to Banda Aceh?' I asked him.*
*'No, never.'*

*'Would you like to?'*

*'No. I'm afraid'.*

*'What of?'*

*'Of meeting someone who knows me. Of knowing. Perhaps they are still there...'*

*'Who?'*

*'Father and mother.'*

*I would have liked to ask him to tell me more, to find out something about his childhood. But then my own fear of remembering flooded back into my mind. It's like a safety valve which kicks in whenever I start to delve into my memories, and find myself staring at the only certain image I have of Haiti, though it isn't even mine; it's a newspaper cutting with a photo of a child crying amidst the rubble. I still have it, in my missal. Secretly, I have always wanted to believe that that child was me, and I have often tried to recognize myself in that weeping face. But I don't cry like that, I have never cried like that. It was dusk when we got back to Amsterdam, and all in all we were glad to see its tangle of lights, to hear its raucous din. We'd had enough of the bucolic emptiness of the Markermeer.*

*20 May*

*Guntur had never told me that he is a great skater! He has even done the Elfstedentocht – all two hundred kilometres of it. When there's no ice, apparently, you train on rollers. Today I followed him on my bike, and by the end I was more exhausted than he was. I haven't done any serious sport since I left the academy; all I have done is wear myself out doing weightlifting. I should take up fencing again. I'm always telling myself to join a club, then laziness gets the upper hand.*

# God's Dog

*22 May*

*Today was the start of the new herring season, as we learned from the papers yesterday. Guntur and I were not going to miss the opportunity of a first tasting. We went to supper on a restaurant-barge belonging to a friend of his from Friesland who makes his own beer and who spends more time drunk than sober. A tankard of wheat beer with* maatjes *herring, the sun setting over the Singel and a wind bearing the sweet scent of grass: it was perfect. To crown it all, Guntur seemed so happy. That man has a kind of ebullience which strikes me as typically eastern, and which must be linked to his capacity for amazement. Nothing seems to dishearten him. He does everything with a kind of lightness which is very refreshing. I myself always feel that I am in the firing line, that I've spent my whole life in the trenches; I see an enemy in everyone who doesn't share my views. That is what I've been trained to do, it's true; that is my trademark. He too was trained as a soldier, of course, but he sees things with more detachment. All in all, for Guntur nothing seems important; at times I find his freedom of thought positively frightening. He makes me feel that, were I to be set free, I wouldn't even dare to leave my cage. Where would I fly to, in this empty, senseless world? I need a mission. When all is said and done, it isn't even a question of faith. Sometime I actually wonder whether I have any faith at all. As my guardian in Bologna used to say to me, 'Salazar, you don't believe in anything except your own survival. But we shall put your defects to good use – along with your good points.' I wonder what they are.*

*25 May*

*Guntur has an amazingly thorough knowledge of the Christian tradition. I don't think I know anything like as much about Islam. He claims that Islam was founded not by Mohammed, but by a sect of monotheistic Christians, Jews and Arabs. It is no coincidence, in his view, that Saint Mark's Gospel is contemporary with the writings of Ibn Ishaq. But then he is syncretism incarnate! Though I'd be interested to hear what an imam thinks of his interpretation of Islam. All in all, I do feel that the Islamic mindset is more inclined than the Christian one to skate over differences. According to their teachings, our prophets were holy men; we treat theirs like so many Bedouin.*

*27 May*

*Today, coming back from prayer, Guntur and I walked through the Vondelpark.*

*'This year the camellias will still be out when the rhododendrons come into flower!' he said, with childlike glee.*

*'It's been a cold spring, so the blossom lasts longer. Look at the Japanese cherry, how frothy the petals are. But if the wind gets up then they'll all fly away, together with the rain. You'll see, it will be as though there'd been a heavy snowstorm. One day I must show you my bulb collection; I grow them in the university greenhouse; I've even managed some cross-breeding.'*

# God's Dog

*28 May*

*Guntur's laboratory is in an old building on the Nieuwe Diep Basin. The windows look straight on to the canal embankment, but to the right of it there is a strip of land occupied by an old disused greenhouse, separated from the entrance by a brick wall; and that was where we left our bicycles, chained to some railings. As we went in, a violent storm was brewing over the Jimeer; the dark sky was flecked with strips of grey and orange, and there was a rumble of distant thunder out at sea. In the restaurant, Guntur had started to tell me more about his experiments. At one point he had looked at the wall clock as though he were waiting for some particular moment in time. Now he had switched on the computer and opened the safe where he kept his data banks. He linked up the hard disk and started the programmes. His large room on the ground floor is crammed with various kinds of apparatus and oddities of the kind he likes to surround himself with, including an old barber's chair.*

*'When I started studying mirror neurons I immediately felt that I was standing at a door that would give me access to a new scientific dimension. Mirror neurons alert us to the existence of an empathy that is all pervasive: they are found in men and monkeys, but we are also discovering them in other animals. So why should they not also exist, in other forms, in plants? Perhaps mirror neurons are fragments of a unity which once suffused all creation. In part, we humans function in the same way as all other beings, and the more contact there is between us, the more we interact. In a word, we think together! And perhaps every being is capable of some form of thought. So your Teilhard de Chardin was right when he talked of a*

88

*noosphere. The whole subject has begun to interest me deeply:*
*mirror neurons might be a step towards the scientific proof of*
*the existence of God; of intelligent design, do you see? The*
*world on its way back to a journey towards the divine!'*

*As he talked, Guntur had his eyes not on me, but on*
*the computer screen where his data was coming up. Now*
*he gestured to me to come closer, as he brought several*
*photographs of a monkey up on to the screen.*

*'This is Django, a young adult chimpanzee we*
*brought back from the forests of Kibele. I started by doing*
*transcranial magnetic stimulation tests, and nuclear scanned*
*encephalographs, in order to locate the mirror neurons. So far*
*unremarkable: we already know that chimpanzees have mirror*
*neurons in the inferior parietal lobe and frontal cortex. But*
*Django had another apparently sensitive area – I could see it*
*vaguely on the scan but had difficulty bringing it into focus.*
*From the reactions to the neuronal stimuli, I began to suspect*
*that it was a sort of Broca's area proper to the chimpanzee.*
*In the human brain, Broca's area is the one concerned with*
*speech. Do you see what this means? That chimpanzees too*
*are capable of speech, or at least they've got the brains for it! I*
*carried on stimulating the area in question, and getting Django*
*to do exercises which I hoped would make it more responsive.*
*Until, one day, the incredible happened: I was adjusting the*
*apparatus when I suddenly realized that Django's usual grunts*
*were now interspersed with clearer sounds; intermittent ones,*
*but definitely phonetic. I taped the lot, and played it back a*
*thousand times. It was then that I made my great discovery:*
*Django speaks Swahili!'*

*Wide-eyed with emotion as he told his tale, Guntur*
*seemed to be keeping the air down in his lungs, as though*
*afraid of running out of breath. Usually so mild, his face, now*

*drained of colour, was twisted into a grimace, his eyebrows suddenly more prominent so that he resembled a mask in an ethnographical museum. He carried on:*

*'He speaks ready-made phrases, mangled and incomplete, but it's definitely Swahili! He must have learned them from the scientists who reared him in Nairobi. Django was born on a nature reserve and has always been in touch with human beings. I wrote to a neurolinguist from the University of Leyden whose name I was given by an imam. Professor Aren De Smet will be coming to see Django next week, but for now the whole business is completely hush-hush. I haven't mentioned it to anyone, apart, obviously to this same neurolinguist from Leyden, who is completely trustworthy and an observant Muslim. Do you realize what atheists would do with this discovery? If Django can speak, then he must have a soul. Does that mean that every living being has a soul? And, if so, what is the difference between life and matter? We have to find out more, and get there first.'*

*As he was speaking, Guntur took a bunch of keys out of the safe.*

*'Come on, let's go and see Django. Then you can make up your own mind.' I followed him through a gate, then down a wrought-iron staircase leading into the basement, from which the greenhouse was entered through a passageway beneath the boundary wall.*

*'You'd better stay on this side of the* terrarium, *you'll be able to hear him well enough from there. He doesn't know you, and he might take fright,' said Guntur as we went into the greenhouse. It had begun to rain, the drops were drumming on the glass and blurring the outlines of the tugboats riding at anchor on the quays of the Nieuwe Diep. The art nouveau building was divided into two by a grille, leaving the*

*chimpanzee ample space to move around on the side nearer the water, which from which it was separated by panes of thick glass. The interior of the enclosure was fitted out with ropes and raised walkways, and there was a sandpit in the middle of the concrete floor. The space was crossed by a channel containing a stream of running water, flowing out into a drain. I took up my post behind the* terrarium *and watched Guntur as he walked forwards towards the cage among the flowering plants. The chimpanzee was sitting on the ground, his back against the grille; he turned his head as he heard Guntur's voice.*

*'*Habari ya jioni, Django*! Habari yako?' I heard Guntur repeat. The chimpanzee seemed intrigued by the showers of rain against the glass; he was looking around him as though puzzled, surprised that he could hear the rain beating but could not see it fall. After some coaxing from Guntur he finally bounded up to the first walkway, which was some two metres above the ground, where he stayed, huddled, fixing Guntur with an alert but distant look. He seemed somehow sad, perhaps even worried. He grunted, yawned, dug around in his fur with his nails until he found something which seemed to be annoying him, removed it and put it in his mouth. He sat still for a few moments, looking listless, then suddenly turned his head to look at Guntur. Now his eyes really did seem to be saying: 'What do you want from me?'*

*'*Habari yako*?' Guntur repeated patiently until Django, goaded by his insistence, suddenly gnashed his teeth in something approaching a laugh, uttered a laboured '*Habari yako*' in return, then leapt down from the walkway and ran off towards the glass wall overlooking the water, where he stayed, looking out to sea, his head bowed. The clouds, which had been moving off eastwards shortly before sunset, now*

*parted, allowing a ray of sun to light up the iron arches of the greenhouse for a moment and cast Django's squat shadow on to the embankment. A shiver ran through me as I caught a brief glimpse of something human in that animal figure. I followed Guntur along the passageway in silence; back in the laboratory, we stood watching the lights come on along the quays.*

*'If Django's speech is nothing more than unwitting imitation on the part of a particularly intelligent animal, then we can send him back out into his pen for children to gawp at. If on the other hand he has a mind of his own, we must learn more about him; we must go to the forests of Kibale and seek out traces of the birth of man!' said Guntur, a slight quiver in his voice.*

*4 June*

*There was hardly a soul in the flower-market this morning. That was where I had arranged to meet Guntur, after prayers. It was going to be a bright day, but a sharp wind was blowing in from the sea, sweeping away the clouds and showering the city with a rain of petals and leaves, leaving them stuck to window panes, to car bonnets. They carpeted the water in the canals, then the current swept them along in slow drifts which got caught under the bridges and against the sides of the barges. The flower-sellers on the Singel did not seem to be in any hurry to open their kiosks; they stood in huddled groups at the doors of the bars, their numb hands in their pockets. I found Guntur rummaging through a box of bulbs.*

*'Look at this,' he said, pointing to a black tuber.*

*'If you were to plant this today, in October it would produce a bright red flower. It's dense with life, even though it looks like*

*a lump of dead matter – in fact, just like the planets orbiting in space. We think of them as arid and burnt-out, but they too may hold the seeds of future life. All that they need to do is find the humus which will make them bloom…'*

*I nodded in agreement, noting that the bulb-seller did not seem to be taking too kindly to Guntur and his rummaging, though Guntur himself seemed impervious to his disapproval; lost in thought, he helped himself to a plastic bag and began to fill it with* Odontonema Strictum.

*'Life and death are so closely intertwined. They seem sealed off from one another, but in fact there is much to tell us that this is not the case. All life is redolent of death. I don't think I mentioned this, but Django arrived here with a mate, Mirah, and she too had grown up in the forests of Kibale. She fell ill, and we sent her back to Kenya, hoping that they might be able to treat her, but she died a few months later. And they sent her body back from Kibale, explaining to us that otherwise Django would go mad: he had to see the corpse in order to be able to mourn. Otherwise, he could never have been able to accept her disappearance. Do you see? Even a chimpanzee has a notion of death. In which case, this bulb too knows that it will flower in October and then die!'*

The vicar closed the exercise-book and sat there for a moment, lost in thought. In the ensuing silence, the airy figures on the frescoed ceiling seemed to be peering down at him. After a time he got up from the desk and went over to the large windows overlooking the gardens. The rhododendrons were all in flower; a gardener was cutting the grass, leaving a strip of lighter green on the lawn. The colours of the rainbow shone through the spray of a fountain as though they were blown glass. The vicar picked up the telephone and said: 'Send in Kowalski.'

The blinding light almost dazzled him. He tried to shade his eyes with his hand, but realized he could not move it. He tried to turn his head, but felt a sharp stab of pain in his nose. Even those few attempts at movement had exhausted him. He now realized that he was tied to a bed, with several tubes attached to his body, and a drip. Yet he felt as though none of this concerned him; he was filled with a sweet, almost euphoric indifference. Someone passed by his bed, and at last the blinds came down. In the half-light he saw a nun walking away. He had been lying there for a long time, or so it seemed to him. He was dimly aware of voices, saw heads bent over him. It was almost dark by the time he was properly awake. Clear-headed at last, he looked around him: he was in a hospital, but it was not San Filippo Neri. The linoleum was green, and the walls blue. Apart from his bed and a formica chair, there was no furniture, not even a cupboard or a bedside table. White light came in through a frosted glass pane in the door. Through the window he could see a row of modern buildings. Suddenly a neon light went on, and two men came in; Salazar recognized the badge of the guardians of the faith on their jackets. The taller one, a sergeant, who was constantly fiddling with his small red moustache, was now plumped down on the only chair; the other one, a lance-corporal, stood behind him, arms crossed. The door opened again, and a nurse came in, removed the tubes from his nose, disconnected the drip and went out again without a word. When the door was shut, the man with the red moustache asked:

'Inspector, have you anything to say to us?'

Salazar tried to prop himself on his elbows to get a better view of his questioner, but was prevented by the straps round his arms and legs.

'I think I must have fallen among abortionists! Sergeant, please untie me! What's going on?'

'That's for you to tell us, inspector…'

'Where are we? What is this place?'

'It's a hospital. And this is the palliative care unit…'

Then Salazar understood. He half-closed his eyes and tried to clench his fists, but even that was beyond him.

'What do you want from me?'

'You are accused of treachery and offences against religion. We want the names of your accomplices in Amsterdam'.

'What do you mean, accomplices? I am a front-line defender of the faith in Amsterdam!' exclaimed Salazar, fully aware that protest would serve no purpose. What he most feared had already happened; they had him cornered.

'In Amsterdam you had a homosexual relationship with an infidel, thereby violating the rule of chastity. Do I have to remind you of number 2351 in Joseph Ratzinger's catechism: the chief sins against chastity are adultery, masturbation, fornication, pornography, prostitution, rape and homosexual acts. Furthermore, you founded a scientistic sect, the so-called Biblical-Koranists. Number 2110, the sin of polytheism and idolatry. Inspector, we want the names of all the missionary priests involved'.

'Sects, idolatry, what utter rubbish! The word is proselytism! Sergeant, these are important matters we're talking about. I am here in Rome on a secret mission and someone tried to kill me,' protested Salazar in a vain attempt to parry the hail of accusations being levelled against him.

'Who are the Darwinists with whom you are plotting against the Church? Who is in the know about the monstrous experiments your accomplice is conducting? The sooner you start to talk, inspector, the sooner we can try and help you…'

The man was looking at him with rheumy eyes which did not seem to fit with his face. He made an angry gesture, then controlled himself.

'Sergeant, get me off this bed and let me speak to my vicar! The appointment is at Sant'Andrea della Valle, Friday, seven o'clock. My registration number is 18246592NLA.'

'We're quite aware of that, inspector…'

'You're barking up the wrong tree, sergeant. I'm on the track of a gang of abortionists who also practise euthanasia. If you don't free me immediately you'll have to answer for the consequences!'

'Salazar, we'll all have to answer for the consequences. But here it's you who's out of order. We know all about you, inspector. We also know that you are a survivor. You escaped the catastrophe which divine providence, in its infinite wisdom, had planned for you. There is no earthquake, no tsunami, which is not part of God's plan, as Sodom and Gomorrah tell us all too clearly. You come from an evil place, inspector, and to such a place, sooner or later, you must return…' At these words, Salazar saw that he was in the hands of a fanatic.

The man with the red moustache stood up. He stood at the foot of the bed and gripped the bars with both his hands. The other man went to the door and gestured towards someone who was waiting in the corridor.

'Inspector, if you won't talk, we for our part have nothing to say to you. Just take a look around. Do you realize where you are? Think about it We'll be back tomorrow.'

As the two guardians of the faith went off, the nurse came back. Blank-faced, she replaced the tube in Salazar's nostrils with practised movements and turned on the drip.

It was dawn when she saw the message arrive on her silenced mobile phone. Outside, the sky was showing signs of whitening. Marta Quinz had left by the back door in order to avoid going past the already open bar. On the patch of waste land near the station illegal immigrants were huddled around fires. The odd burst of laughter and barking dogs could be head above the din of the traffic. Several prostitutes were still standing around the petrol pumps, but the lorries coming off the by-pass were no longer stopping. Marta took a roundabout route, changing buses three times and doing the last stretch on foot to rejoin her associates; the first thing she did when she went into the backroom, breathless from her exertions, was to look out of the window on to the road.

'Where's Mirko?' she asked the man who was standing under the naked bulb that was hanging from the ceiling; his face was carved out by the glancing light, and she could not see his eyes.

'Through there,' he said. The fair-haired man came in; he hesitated to look Marta in the eye and bit his lip. Then he took a seat at the table, banging his elbows down on to its surface.

'What's happened? Is there any news?' the woman asked.

'No. I know nothing. We didn't see them arrive.'

'They must have been following you!'

'In that case they can't have realized that we were following the lorry; and they didn't see me get out of the car. But there's something that doesn't quite add up. When the two police vehicles arrived, Boris was sitting in front, but not in the driving seat, and Ciro was in the back; clearly, neither of them was at the wheel. So the police must have noticed that the driver wasn't there, but oddly enough they didn't look for him. They surrounded the car and stayed put. And it was there that the men in the other two police cars found them when they arrived on the scene, sirens blaring. There was no road block.'

'Then they could be on our trail. They're biding their time.

Perhaps they're letting us carry on the better to jump on us when we come out into the open!'

'That's not impossible. But there's another possibility. Maybe Boris got into the driving seat in the service area in order to come and get me. I heard the car door open and close as I moved off. If that's what happened, the police may have thought that everyone was there, and that's why they didn't look any further. Anyway, the fact is that this basement isn't safe any more. If we want to carry on, we'll have to move everything into the little house in town.'

'We can't, it's too far away!'

'We have no alternative. Do we want to carry on?'

Marta was walking up and down between the table and the door, but she kept her eye on the window.

'Pablo, what do you think?' The man who had been keeping his distance now came to sit opposite the fair-haired man. He ran a finger through his beard before he spoke.

'We carry on! We can't just let everything drop. We'll never have another chance like this. Just think of the repercussions! Boris and Ciro will manage somehow. The cops have got nothing on them. The car was clean, properly registered in Ciro's name. We've never used it for anything dodgy, not even for removals.'

Marta too pulled up a chair and joined them at the table, heaving a heavy sigh which, in the sudden silence, sounded almost like a shout.

'We carry on!' she repeated, more quietly, shaking the men's hands.

# III

He vaguely recognized the face he now saw beside him, but he couldn't place it. Then he recognized it from the rosary. The woman gestured to him to keep silent. She had two fingers firmly on the drip, and now she squeezed it.

'Listen to me carefully. Your life is at stake.'

'What are you doing here?'

'Don't worry about that. Just listen to me.'

'First, just undo these straps.'

'I can't. Don't you understand, we're being watched.'

'Why should I trust you?'

'Don't, then, if that's how you want it. Just listen.' The woman gave an exaggerated sigh and proceeded wearily with her explanations.

'I'm here for a terminally ill patient. In the next room. Last night I opened the wrong door and came in here. That's how I recognized you.'

'So it was you who helped Bonardi die?'

'Yes, it was me.'

'Or was the old man in San Filippo Neri Davide Zago?'

At these words, her expression darkened. 'I don't know what you're talking about,' she said, looking distinctly uneasy as she did so.

'Davide Zago, Ivan's father, wanted by the papal police for performing backstreet abortions,' insisted Salazar, feeling that at last he had touched upon something solid amidst the surrounding fog. The woman hesitated, and bit her lip; she knew she should say nothing, but she could not contain herself.

'How do you know about all this?'

'I was given the task of exposing Davide Zago and laying a trap for his son. That is why I was keeping an eye on the hospital, pretending to be a pilgrim priest.' She seemed relieved, but then glanced nervously at the panel in the door behind her, reflected in the glass.

'Davide Zago died last month in the military hospital on the Caelian Hill. He was arrested at Filippo Neri after the last sweep. We weren't able to hide him. Those swine kept him hostage to get Ivan to give himself up to the police. They may have tortured him. He will certainly have suffered greatly as he died. The family weren't allowed to take possession of the body.' It came out all in one breath; it was a story she'd never put into words before, and she was surprised that she was able to sum it up so neatly. Salazar listened in disbelief.

'I fail to understand such fury against a medical abortionist. There are so many of them. What had this Ivan done that was so serious?'

'Ivan was one of us. But when they arrested him he let himself be bribed. They'd sentenced him to ten years, so he agreed to perform abortions on the seminary girls.'

'The seminary girls? And who might they be?'

'You've certainly led a sheltered life, inspector. The seminary girls are the whores who serve the curia. You know how it is, your friends don't like doing it with a contraceptive; anyway, they're worth their weight in gold around these parts. So Ivan would perform abortions on them, and the judge commuted his sentence into house arrest. But Ivan kept a careful record of all the abortions, with videos and samples of DNA. Then he fled to Switzerland and began blackmailing the curia, so they took his father hostage. But this is no time for idle chitchat.'

'I see. Things are becoming a bit clearer. But what do you want from me?'

'I want to get you out of here.'

'That's big of you. Alive or dead?'

'This is no time for banter. Just listen carefully. In a moment or two I shall be stunning you with this.' The woman unscrewed a tube from the bed and showed Salazar an object hidden inside it.

'It's an electric stun gun. We use them to induce cardiac arrest; when used on the terminally ill, they're fatal; all it will do to you is cause you to lose consciousness.'

'And it was this which left those two black marks on Bonardi's chest?'

'Exactly. No one would ever associate such marks with a stun gun.'

'My congratulations. You had me there. Did you realize who I was?'

'Not straight away. But caution is second nature to us.'

'That's some organization you've got there. How do you chose which patients should be killed? How much do they pay you to die?'

The woman looked around her, uncertain whether to talk or to remain silent. But she found Salazar's provocations impossible to resist.

'We don't kill them, we save them! And we don't ask for money, though they can give us money, if they want. We use it to finance the backstreet abortions. It's the families who contact us. We have ourselves registered as visiting relatives and we go and live in relatives' houses, to avoid suspicion. The relatives themselves go to stay in our safe houses while we are getting things sorted out. Sometimes we have to do a bit of jiggery-pokery to make things seem more plausible.'

'Like photographs in family albums?'

'Down to the last detail. We know your methods!'

'And you go from hospital to hospital, so as to keep a low profile'.

'That's right, we're constantly on the move, even from city to city'.

'When did you realize who I was?'

'It was pure chance. The morning when you went into the Bonardi flat, I'd forgotten my tube pass. So I went back, and when I arrived on the landing I heard noises. I lay in wait for you in the street and saw you come out.'

'One can never be too careful…'

'Listen, we haven't got much time. When I've done the business with the stun gun, your pulse rate will be too low to register on the cardiac monitor, so the alarm will go off, and the flying squad will take you into the recovery room. That's where we come on the scene. We'll put you into a bogus ambulance and get you out of here, and we'll have to sedate you, to get through the check points.'

'But why do you want to save my life, Mrs… what should I call you? Bonardi? Loiacono?' An expression of unease flickered over her face again.

'I see you haven't wasted any time…'

'I'm a policeman…'

'As you will have suspected, Loiacono is a false name, too.'

'Well, I thought so. But it could be a clue.'

She bit her lip. 'It could indeed,' she said thoughtfully.

Then, reverting to her previous briskness:

'You could call me "death's angel". Isn't that what you call us?'

'All right, death's angel. What do you want in exchange?'

'Information. About the ceremony on Easter Day. About where the marksmen will be positioned; how many plainclothes-policemen will be there, how to recognize them, what time will the pope be arriving on the podium, who will be with him, the route of the popemobile… that kind of thing.'

Salazar thought that it might be as well to make the bogus Mrs. Bonardi believe that he had something to divulge. He tried to think who among the police had laid that trap for him; perhaps some corrupt secret service agent who wanted to trip him up? Perhaps his anti-reformist activism had irked someone? Or perhaps, more simply, he had trodden on the toes of some bad egg who had friends in high places?

'And how can I be sure that it won't be you who kills me?'

'You can't. But if you stay here, you'll die anyway. Perhaps as soon as this evening. With this,' the woman said, pointing to the tube with the drip she was still gripping between her fingers. 'Between shifts, someone will come and inject another liquid into the bag.'

'Is that what they do?'

'We've seen all sorts.'

Salazar was exhausted. Now he could scarcely speak; he felt extremely weak, and his head was spinning. He looked the woman in the eye, seeking a sign of some emotion. Her mouth looked like a bloodless wound cut into the white flesh. She waved her hands around vaguely, one clutching the tube and the other the rosary, as though to tell him to hurry up.

'I can't stay long, inspector!'

'The deal is done, death's angel… I'm ready!' Salazar said

after a pause.

'Good. This is what will happen: as soon as the relatives start leaving, I'll put the stun gun under your armpit. The cardiac monitor alarm won't go off immediately. I'll have time to get away.'

Salazar looked towards the blue square of window; in the spring sky, the first cold stars were coming out. Below, he could picture the Roman streets, the warm colour the buildings took on in the evening light. He felt a sudden stabbing in his chest, gave a hoarse gasp and lost consciousness.

Guntur was running along the edge of the Oosterpark towards the Nieuwe Diep. Only too late had he realized that that man was not Aren De Smet. He should have had his suspicions even at the station: when he met him on the platform where the train from Leyden had pulled in, De Smet was coming out of the subway, so he could not have just come off that train. Furthermore, he had nothing of the university professor about him, with that strange little leather bag on his shoulder. He was too elegant, and too athletic. Also, he was too African, too dark for what he was supposed to be. He even had an issue of the *Nieuwe Afrikaanse Courier* in his pocket. They had gone straight to the laboratory. Guntur had managed to get Django to speak while the man from Leyden listened from behind the *terrarium*. Then he had come forward, had pulled a tape recorder out of his coat pocket and held out the microphone towards the chimpanzee, attaching it to one of the bars. Guntur had objected: he didn't want any recordings. The African had smiled politely and reassured him, explaining that he was making a recording so that he would be able to analyse the sounds made by the chimpanzee on his equipment. He assured Guntur that he had no intention of using the films for any other purpose, but he would leave him the tape recorder if that was what Guntur preferred.

'If you like, you could come to my institute with the recording and help me while I scan it. Such a scan will enable me to locate the phonatory organs with extreme precision, together with the muscle movements and their link-up with the brain. Of course, an electroencephalogram would be even better; but I don't suppose that would be easy.'

'I've already tried. But I had to sedate him, and as a result his reactions were different: he couldn't speak,' Guntur had explained, now somewhat reassured, though there was still something which worried him. It was indeed Swahili that the man had been speaking when he talked to Django; Guntur had recognized a number of words. But the chimpanzee had been strangely nervous; he had made agitated gestures, waving his paws in front of his face, beating his chest and baring his teeth, as he did when he was irritated. Then he had climbed up on to the highest walkway and expressed his apparent disapproval of the man, who then seemed to lose interest, leaving the tape recorder running and looking around him. Guntur had thought that he was looking for a safer place to rest his microphone, and he had gone to the laboratory to look for some adhesive tape. On his return, he found his guest apparently measuring the width of the grille, casting glances in the direction of the fire escape running up the outer wall of the warehouses which bordered the first stretch of the canal. Seeing Guntur come in, the man had ceased his observations and came towards him, clearly enthusiastic.

'It's a sensational discovery. That was Swahili he was speaking, no two ways about it! Of course they're just random ready-made phrases with no logic to them; but the animal can clearly speak!' he said, almost squeaking with excitement as he picked up his tape recorder. That's odd, Guntur had thought; it hadn't seemed to him that Django had uttered a single word in the man's hearing, only grunted and bellowed. But then he thought that perhaps the chimp had spoken when he had gone out to get the adhesive tape. As promised, the man had then handed over the tape recorder, though he'd asked him to think about his suggestion.

'I'm sure that you'd be interested in the work we are doing at Leyden. Shall we talk it over this evening over a good *rijstafel*?' he suggested with a cautious smile.

Guntur had accepted. They had arranged to meet that evening at 19.30 at the Java Satay, on the Nassaukade, near the Leidesplein. The linguist had told him that he had a few things to do in Amsterdam and wanted to catch the 21.17 train back to Leyden. It had not occurred to Guntur to wonder why someone intending to catch a train should choose a restaurant so far from the station; now he saw how slow-thinking he had been. Soaked to the skin, he ran over the slippery cobbles through the fine rain, his chest tight with effort, his legs aching; such few passers-by as there were stood aside in some alarm to let him pass. At last he arrived on the quay and went over the bridge which led to the university. The campus lights lit up the broad open space between the modern buildings which had sprung up around the old nineteenth-century complex. Guntur went through the gate and took the path to the brick building. The door had not been tampered with. He turned the key hurriedly in the lock and deactivated the alarm. Everything seemed to be as he had left it. It was now raining heavily, huge clouds were rolling in over the Nieuwe Diep, and water and land seemed to have merged into a single greenish haze. Guntur ran into the laboratory, pausing to take his ritual knife down from the wall; it was a *kris* from Bali he'd bought in an antique shop, more to play the part of a real Indonesian than for any other reason. He didn't even know how to use it, but he felt safer with a weapon in his belt. The rain was lashing on to the glass of the greenhouse, making a deafening roar. There too all seemed to be in order. The campus lights cast only a faint glimmer on the grass, and the pavement outside the lab was now almost in complete darkness; the building itself was sunk in shadow. Django didn't notice Guntur as he came in: as always when there was a heavy downpour, he was leaning up against the glass overlooking the water, gripping the grille and casting occasional nervous glances around him. Guntur took a few steps towards him; he didn't want to frighten him, so he paused for a few moments. Just as he had noticed that the African's little microphone was still attached to the grille, a sudden explosion shattered the glass. The chimp howled and ran for cover, but another four shots sent him tumbling down into the sand pit. Guntur ran for the door which led to the quay and saw the man from Leyden on the far bank, putting away his gun. He jumped down the embankment and ran along to the end of the quay in the lee of a wall. He didn't know what he was going to do, but sheer blind rage drove him to pursue the false De Smet. He knew that bit of asphalt-covered earth like the back of his hand; at the end of it was a concrete jetty with moorings for the barges. The African would have to go that way to get back to the shore. Guntur crouched down and unsheathed his knife.

It was still raining heavily. The lighthouse at the mouth of the canal was flashing, and a tugboat was sounding its siren in the mist. The bogus De Smet was running among the mooring-posts, leap-frogging over the hawsers. In that downpour, he couldn't see within an inch of his nose, but he was sure that

Guntur was around there somewhere. He had put down his bag and was holding his gun at the ready. Guntur saw him approaching, climbed up to the edge of the asphalt-covered patch of ground and was about to leap on him. But the African had slipped and fallen, so he could see his attacker looming up out of the mist. Twisting this way and that, Guntur positioned himself firmly and fixed his gaze on the wall of water which now obscured the African's silhouette. This wall of water was now approaching, taking on human form, becoming arms and legs. Guntur let fly a downward blow, but missed. Meanwhile the African had picked up his gun and pulled the trigger, but lost his balance at the crucial moment, so that the bullet ricocheted across the concrete. Guntur repositioned himself, drew back his arm and tried again: an upward blow this time, aimed to land where it would kill. The tip of his knife sliced through the folds of the African's sodden overcoat and bit into his flesh. The man put one hand to his stomach, staggered and fell to his knees, but, making one final effort, managed to hit Guntur on the head, using his pistol as a club. Guntur's howl of pain was lost in the louder howling of the wind. For a moment everything went black and he seemed to lose consciousness. He felt blood from the wound pouring into his eyes. Seizing the moment, the African got to his feet and made a run for it, dragging himself along the asphalt-covered dyke towards the bridge over the motorway; but Guntur was in hot pursuit, right on his heels. The African was limping, his stomach clearly causing him severe pain, his strength ebbing away. Now he was struggling back up the asphalt-covered patch of ground where he had fallen. Guntur caught up with him on the bank, under the piers of the bridge. He flung himself upon the man; holding the *kris* in both hands, he brought it down between the man's shoulders; the African saw it glint briefly before he felt the blow, which took his breath away. He dropped his gun and fell heavily to the ground. In one last bid for escape, he was now dragging himself along on his elbows, then started thrashing around with his knees on the algae-infested embankment, his hands towards the canal, vainly seeking assistance from the scummy mass of water that opened up before him as he watched his blood mingle with the rain in the Nieuwe Diep; then he allowed himself to slip down from the quay and sank into the water without a sound. Thoroughly dazed, his face dripping with blood and his head throbbing with pain, Guntur got to his feet and peered through the rain-pocked ripples at the body of the man from Leyden as the current carried it away.

He went back to the greenhouse in search of Django, but it was too late: the chimpanzee was lying lifeless on the blood-stained sand. Now that he was dead, he had once more become the animal that he had always been, his face that of a chimpanzee and nothing more. The chink through which Guntur had glimpsed a mind in the creature had now closed up for good: millions of years had been sucked back into the void. He shook himself: he was in danger there, he had to get away. Whoever had put the bogus De Smet on his trail would not stop there. He picked up a roll of oilskin he kept in the laboratory, bound up the wound to his head, concealing it beneath a sailor's cap, threw the false De Smet's hard disks and computer into a sports bag and set off in the rain towards the station. Once in the dimly-lit entrance hall he felt distinctly uneasy, and kept on peering nervously over his shoulder. The departure of the African's train to Leyden was up on the departure board. He joined the queue at the booking-office without the faintest idea of where he was going to go. When his turn came he hesitated, then finally told the irritated man in the ticket-office that he wanted to go to Antwerp, where he had an old friend from college days, though he hadn't the faintest idea of his address. The train slid out into the night, grinding along at a leisurely pace as though it didn't dare to proceed more speedily amidst the downpour which was drumming heavily against its windows. The 22.30 Thalys for Paris stopped at Rotterdam, Antwerp and Brussels; it was the one used by the art dealers who came to the Dutch auctions, who would take the fast train home after celebrating a successful deal with a good meal. But that evening there was hardly anyone on board, apart from a few Japanese, buried amidst enormous suitcases, their maps of Europe spread out upon the table. Guntur cast a brief glance at their synthetic raincoats, leaned his head up against the window and fell asleep.

Bogdan always boarded the train at the last minute. He would buy a ticket for Schiphol, and make sure that it was checked by the inspector. Then he had time, until Rotterdam, to eye up any dealer who had had a good day; but the timing had to be calculated down to the last second, and he had to jump out pretty smartly when the moment came. He had noticed the man with the sports bag immediately; that man was clearly ill at ease. There were only four people in the carriage, all facing the engine. His designated victim was the last one near the door. Standing in the corridor, Bogdan made a show of hanging his overcoat from the coat hook. He had his back to the man and watched his reflection in the window. The outlines of the other passengers were reflected in the black, rain-streaked glass. Further on he could see a foot, a suitcase on the luggage rack, an open newspaper shaken by the rocking of the train. The door to the corridor was closed. All that was needed was a well-aimed punch; then he would grab the bag and jump out of the train. The ticket-inspector had already been round, and Bogdan had made a point of showing him his ticket seated in the first empty place he'd come upon; then he had walked slowly through the train, looking for a possible victim. He waited patiently until the red lights of the Rotterdam wind farm came into view among the greenhouses. He took down his coat and slowly put it on. The corridor itself was empty; the odd arm protruded from a seat, the odd head could be seen leaning against a window, but no one was looking his way; there was no movement behind him, either. He crept towards the seat where the man with the sports bag was sitting and prepared to deliver his blow almost without looking. But Guntur, awoken by a sudden jolt, had raised his head, reacted speedily and avoided it: leaning to one side, thrusting his feet against him, he pushed Bogdan violently against the window. Bogdan fell on top of him and forced him to stretch out on the seat, pressing his knees against the man's chest. Wide-eyed with fear, Guntur tried to cry out, fending his assailant off with outstretched hands. In desperation, Bogdan aimed repeated blows at his victim's face, until he saw, with satisfaction, that his nose was bleeding. Then, without a moment's hesitation, he seized the bag, reaching the step just as the puff of compressed air caused the door to open. The inside of the carriage was lit up by the lights of the station awning; the rain continued to pour down, drumming on the metal roof. There was a scuffle, someone shouted out '*Au secours*!' Bogdan jumped down on to the platform and ran off.

Ivan's phone call had stirred up old memories. She looked in the bathroom mirror and tidied her hair, as though she wanted to look decent should he happen to be outside the door and suddenly walk in. She had been ill-advised to tell him everything; now she was putting him in danger too. In any case, Ivan himself was half-crazed by a desire for revenge: he might do something rash. But she had been unable to help herself. At times she thought she heard affection in his voice; or was she just imagining things? Could he really be completely indifferent to her? He too must surely still feel something. Even if she hadn't heard from him for almost two years. Of course, he had other worries: his escape, his non-appearance in court, and then his father's awful death. By now he would certainly have found another woman, and the thought of Ivan looking tenderly at someone else was more than she could bear. She could no longer remember how his voice sounded when he spoke lovingly to her. Yet they had been happy together; perhaps it had been the rape which had ruined everything. No, that's not right, she thought, everything was already over when that happened. Perhaps, though, without that horror story, they would have been able to start afresh; everything could have been as it had been before. The nearest 'before' for which she still felt nostalgia was so far away! Now she was running headlong towards the 'after'. Only the 'after' could save her from the unbearable 'now'. But how had he been able so easily to forget her? She couldn't have been very important to him if he had been able to detach himself from her so light-heartedly. Yet what did she know about Ivan's deepest feelings? They had not been able to communicate during the ten months she had spent in prison, and seeing each other during the other three years of probation had not been easy, either. It had always all been such a rush, and they had always been terrified of being caught. Perhaps he was avoiding her for her own good; at all events, that was what Marta liked to think. So why did she persist in wanting to see him now? To help him, that was what she told herself at the time. But he was difficult: it was as though he came to those meetings on sufferance. She had hoped that she might be able to wipe out the past by her mere presence, but Ivan had his mind on other things. He was making plans for his escape; she was not in the forefront of his mind. At the time, she had had to make do with that; she would have to make do with that now as well. Ivan wasn't coming back to her; he was lost to her for good. He was as caught up in his hatred as she was in her loneliness.

The common grave lay on the other side of a lawn running along the west side of the hill. Ivan went up to the yellow stone with the dates of the earliest and most recent burials carved into it. A light wind blew through the grass, ruffling the cypresses that overlooked the tomb. On the slope that ran down towards the road, yellow mimosa bushes were in flower, giving off a delicate scent of early spring. He thought back to the last time he had seen his mother alive, and that was many years ago by now. It was a summer's day, he'd just come back from an afternoon at the seaside with Marta. He remembered her mild look, her eyes distorted behind thick glasses, the vague smile she put on in an attempt to please him and above all not let him see that she was worried. At least she had died quickly. Whereas his father... Who knows where they had dumped his corpse? More than the pain, it was the thought of the fear his father must have felt that caused Ivan such gut-wrenching fury. And the loneliness. Locked up in prison, watched over like a murderer, there in his filthy cell. Ivan tried to get these images out of his head, but they kept coming back to him as though he had been a physical witness to his father's suffering. In fact, he knew nothing of his father's death. When he had been taken into the hospital on the Caelian Hill, he hadn't been able to see his own doctor; he tried to decipher the reports of the military doctors to get some idea of his condition. The telephone conversations he had had with Ivan had not been reassuring; not much was said. He had talked like a medical chart, addressing him in the polite form; he knew that his conversations with Ivan were recorded. The police had allowed them hoping they might reveal something about Ivan's whereabouts. He remembered how wretched he'd felt during that time. He'd desperately wanted to go to see his father, but that would have meant another stint in prison, and this time there would have been no reprieve. At least this way they would leave his father in peace. He would never have thought that they would take it out on him, an old man who was already serving a death sentence. How could they be so cruel? But it was that fanatic Novak who was the wild beast among them, it was he who spurred on the all the rest; he was an obsessive, and his underlings were ready to obey him in order to further their own careers. Ultimately Ivan had decided to go back, to get himself arrested. He had been on the road when he had received Boris's phone call. His father had died, perhaps some days ago. A routine letter had arrived at his old address. The date of death was uncertain. Novak would have liked to keep it secret, in order to lure Ivan to Rome, but the bureaucrats at the papal registry office had overridden him, powerful though he was. Ivan dried his eyes on the back of his hand. He picked a daisy and threw it onto the slab of stone that covered his mother's tomb.

From the basement in which he now found himself, Salazar could see a dense grove of pine trees, a strip of sand and the iron gateway to a villa. All he knew of his whereabouts was that he was on the coast. A patch of sky, overcast but bright, a quiet road, a lot of dust. Salazar didn't know what day it was, but from his calculations it should be Easter Saturday. The only noise filtering in from the outside was the chirping of sparrows. Suddenly, he was deafened by the sound of a plane landing; the runway must be extremely close. It was probably early morning, because there was a smell of fresh bread in the air. He looked down at himself and saw that he was wearing a track suit and trainers. All there was in the room was the camp-bed on which he had been lying, and a bottle of water, on the floor. Beyond the wall he could hear the cackle of a radio. Suddenly the door opened and four people came in, the bogus Chiara Bonardi and three others with stockings over their faces. They pushed him into the next-door room and sat him down at a table; one of the three stood opposite him with a pen and paper, the others took up positions behind him. Salazar looked around him as best he could, trying not to move his head. He was in the living room of a holiday home, but the furnishings seemed past their prime: he noted the faded nautical motifs on the wallpaper, some blue pottery covered with dust, a large fish-shaped vase with a chipped rim. There was a divan beneath the tall window and a small bamboo table between two non-matching chairs. The wrought-iron table at which he was seated had a glass top covered with an old discoloured sheet. There were patches of mould on the brick floor. Four rucksacks were piled up against the wall near the door.

'Don't strain yourself, there's nothing to see!' said the man opposite him. The other two were peering out through the blinds. A car drove up, and the driver switched off the engine. They nodded, as though to confirm that everything was under control.

The woman went round to the other side of the table.

'Now you must tell us everything, inspector. That was our agreement!' she said in a rasping tone, looking distinctly nervous by now.

'I'll do my best,' said Salazar. He was in no position to foil their plans; all he could do was string them along, but his subterfuge had to be carefully considered, bearing in mind what he had read on the phone belonging to the hit-man who'd been sent to kill him. The members of the brigade almost certainly knew something already. It should be enough to tweak the truth a little in order to seem credible and lead them into making some mistake.

'Where are the marksmen? We've located four positionings around the portico, but we know there are others.'

'Yes, there are two others, one on the Leonine Walls and one on the roof of the Galleria Aurora.' It wasn't true, but it was plausible.

'Any others?'

'They usually post them between the statues on the façade of the basilica.' This was invention pure and simple.

'What about plainclothes-men, how many will there be? How will we recognize them?'

'I don't know how many there'll be, but you can recognize them by the yellow buttons on the collars of their shirts.' That, at least, was true. But Salazar knew that during an event as momentous as the canonization of a pope, nothing and no one would be recognizable. The police would mingle with the pilgrims, the friars, the nuns and even the sick in search of a miracle.

'What about the podium. Do you know when it will be ready?'

'No, but usually everything is in place before the maximum security measures come into force. The workmen have to be out of the area so that the papal guard can make their inspections. Not even the pope can enter it without their authorization. So I presume that the podium will be completely finished by the evening of the day before the ceremony.' At least that made good sense, even if it was not very informative.

'And who keeps watch over the place during the night?'

'I don't know about such details. All I know is that the night patrol comes on at midnight, when the Swiss Guards finish their shift.' From his time at police school, Salazar knew that the six o'clock changing of the guard in Saint Peter's Square was just a show put on for tourists; the real change took place at midnight. But the real guards were not those who relieved one another outside the basilica; there were many others in readiness behind the wall of the colonnade.

'What about the telecameras? Where will they be?' That was something else he could tell them. Those telecameras were indestructible. Perhaps if they realized what they were up against they might lose heart and give up the whole endeavour.

'Under the colonnade, every ten metres. Four on the façade of the basilica and one at the top of the obelisk.'

The man who was questioning him looked away for a moment. The others were discussing something in low voices over a map they had spread out at the other end of the table. Chiara Bonardi was shaking her head, indicating a point on it with her finger. Salazar took advantage of the moment to take a closer look at the man's face behind the stocking mask. He saw a beard, but that was all he could make out; the stocking distorted his other features.

'What time does the papal procession arrive?' the man persisted, seeing himself being looked at. Salazar had a perfect memory of the pope's prospective movements; that was what he had paid most attention to when he'd studied the cadet's mobile phone. Then he remembered the leaflets and posters he'd seen in Saint Peter's Square, and came out with something he hoped was plausible.

'There isn't going to be a procession. On such occasions the pope comes out of the basilica on foot. He has to be on the pódium by eleven, so I imagine he will be going down the flight of stairs around ten forty-five. He's usually accompanied by the papal prefect, the secretary of state, the chief of the papal police, the heads of the congregations and the commander-in-chief of Propaganda Fide. But they don't go up to the altar; they stay down on the lower part of the podium; and they will already be in their places when the pope arrives. The only person who is always with him is the deacon.'

'Where will Benedict XVI's sarcophagus be placed?' There had been nothing about this on the cadet's phonecard, so Salazar had to improvise. Even though he had been just a boy when Karol Wojtyla had been canonized, he remembered the event, which he had watched on television.

'It will be borne on to the podium and placed in front of the altar, probably leaving the basilica at the same time as the pope.' That was fairly plausible. The man who was questioning him was taking notes, tapping his biro nervously over the paper. The others were now folding up the map and putting on their rucksacks.

'This had better all be true, inspector, or we'll be taking you back to the hospital! And your mates will see to it that you meet your maker!' Salazar nodded, giving him a defiant look.

'Now we're going to have to blindfold you and take you to another hiding place.'

'Can I refuse?'

'I don't think so. It won't be for long, forty-eight hours at most.'

'Perhaps it would be better if you killed me straight away.'

'We won't be doing that; you're of no interest to us.'

Salazar was put into the back of a van with his hands tied behind his back and a towel around his head. The driver set off at some speed, but had to brake continually to negotiate sharp curves. Short climbs, followed by short descents, suggested that the van was going over bridges; sometimes it jolted along what might have been a gravelled surface. There was a smell of dust. He was taken out of the van in an underground car park and taken to another basement, in part of an old garage; there was a smell of petrol, and old tyres. A room with the camp-bed that had come with them in the van; two small windows with frosted glass, and bars. A metal door led into a lavatory; there were oil stains on the floor, and piles of sawdust. One of the men freed his hands, but tied his feet together with a bicycle chain. Before going out, the woman put a bag on the floor. 'Something to eat and drink', she said, darting him a sympathetic glance. He made a move to go towards her, but the bicycle chain prevented him.

'Wait...' said Salazar. The woman paused on the threshold.

'I wanted to thank you. I think you've saved my life...'

'It's nothing...' she said, embarrassed; then she looked away and went out of the room, closing the door behind her.

Trains full of pilgrims were arriving at Stazione Termini one after the other. Hundreds of monks and nuns were thronging the platforms and wandering off into the station entrance. Men and women of every conceivable hue were calling to each other in a Babel of tongues, waving the flags of their various countries and forming orderly lines, their vast array of uniforms and insignia attesting to the Church's awesome power. Salazar looked like a beggar in his tattered track suit and trainers. He wandered around the station in search of an internet point. It had taken him several hours to free himself, patiently working the bicycle chain against the metal door of the lavatory; but the hard part had been getting out of the basement. Luckily he had heard voices on the other side of the wall, and had called out. He had been heard by an electrician who'd come down into the basement to do some repairs, who had told the watchman, who had come down with the spare key. Salazar told him that he'd recently rented the storeroom and locked himself in by mistake, then made himself scarce, not leaving the man time to wonder at his stupidity. At the bus station he had at last seen an Italcom sign, and gone in. He hadn't a penny on him, so was obliged to wait until someone went off leaving some credit on the computer. An Indian seminarist had grasped his predicament, possibly having been in the same position himself, and let him take his place. There were still twenty minutes left on the phonecard. The first thing Salazar did was to check his emails. He found a message from Guntur.

*Dear Domingo,*

*I got your message just today because I spent all yesterday in a seminary out of town. All's well here, no news. Or rather, to tell the truth, I feel slightly worried: I have the feeling I'm being watched. Yesterday I thought I saw the flash of cameras from the other side of the glass, though it might just have been a sailor from one of the barges taking a photo of the quay for a souvenir. But then I have another worry; I must be overdoing things. I was afraid that Django might start talking in front of Henk, the keeper who comes to feed him and clean his cage. Then I realized that Henk probably wouldn't understand that the chimp was doing anything other than grunting. Tomorrow I'm expecting this Aren De Smet from Leyden. Meanwhile, I carry on encouraging Django with recordings of voices in Swahili and other exercises. I'm eager to get on with my research, but I need time to perfect certain experiments, and it's complicated doing all this in secret. It would be good to be able to talk to colleagues, and consult scientific journals. But I'm staking my all on this neurolinguist, and I'm expecting material from America which might prove decisive. How are you getting on in Rome? I don't suppose that you can tell me much about your mission. I'd thought of asking for a visa and coming to visit you in May, if you're not back by then, that is. It would be good to see you here when the first new catch of herring of the year arrives; we could go to supper again with my Friesian friend. Apparently his place has become all the rage with yuppies and intellectuals and other toffs. But I discovered it when it was just a rough-and-ready bar, with paper tablecloths and sawdust on the floor. I wonder if Rik still gets drunk now that his place is in the good restaurant guide!*

*My warmest greetings, Guntur.*

The message was four days old. Salazar deleted it. All communication with Guntur now had to cease; he might get him into trouble, and put someone on his own trail. By now his emails would certainly be checked. But was Guntur really being watched? If they'd got their hands on him, they would certainly also have located Guntur, whose experiments would upset a lot of people. Salazar feared for his friend; he would have liked to put him on his guard. Then another alarming thought struck him. He googled Guntur Pertiwi, University of Amsterdam. What came up was a photograph of a burned-out ruin on the Nieuwe Diep.

*On Tuesday evening, during the storm which hit the whole north Dutch coast, causing flooding and serious damage, a fire broke out in the Amsterdam University Complex, probably caused by the collapse of a high-tension pylon. The building which houses the biological research laboratory run by Professor Guntur Pertiwi and the adjacent greenhouse were completely destroyed. The fire brigade was on the spot within minutes, but a high wind prevented them from bringing the flames under control. Their situation was made more difficult by the nearby presence of reservoirs containing diesel for the river barges which moor at the adjacent quay. During the night the fire also spread to this same quay, destroying a barge and causing the reservoirs to explode. Only at first light were the firemen able to approach the quay and train seawater on to the building, which was by now a mere burnt-out hull. There do not seem to have been any victims on the barge, which was carrying sand and gravel. However, while work was going on to make the place safe, the charred body of a man was found at the foot of the embankment, together with that of a monkey. The body has not yet been identified, but is presumed to be that of Professor Pertiwi. The monkey is undoubtedly to be identified as the chimpanzee Django, originally from the Kibale Nature Reserve in Kenya, on whom Professor Pertiwi was conducting various experiments. There do not seem to be any other victims. The police have opened enquiries into the cause of the fire.*

The fair-haired man rolled up the shutters, picked up the newspapers and went back into the bar. The coffee-machine was already on. He poured some coffee into the filter-paper, put it in place and pressed the switch; what he wanted was the smell of coffee. He spread the newspaper out over the counter and put his cup on it. Every so often he glanced out into the street, unable to resist the urge to check that nothing unusual was happening. He saw the dustcart, the wholesaler who served the greengrocer, the night-watchman from the nearby lawyer's office getting on his scooter, the seven o-clock bus. Between the colourfully-packaged Easter eggs he could also see the ramparts of the Vatican bristling with white and yellow flags. Then he felt his mobile buzzing in his pocket; he pulled it out and snapped it open. The number was that of a public phone box.

'Are you alone?'

'Yes. Who's speaking?'

'It's me, Ivan…'

'Ivan! Where are you?'

'Here in Rome. I've just arrived.'

'Are you completely mad? They're still after you here!'

'I know. And I'm still after them. Zladek Novak is on the hit list.'

'Ivan, do you realize what's going on?'

'Marta has told me everything. Your madcap plans will cause utter bedlam, and I'll take advantage of it to murder that swine.'

'Leave it to us. He'll be made mincemeat of along with Benedict XVIII…'

'No, he might not go up on to the podium and escape the explosion. And anyway, I want to kill him with my own hands. I want to see the terror in that one eye when he sees me pointing a pistol at his head.'

The fair-haired man sat bolt-upright in his chair. He looked out of the window at the passers-by, hoping they didn't include an imminent customer.

'Do the others know you're here?' he asked, raising his hand and putting it on the coffee-machine.

'Only you and Marta. The fewer the better.'

'You do realize that you might be putting a spanner in the entire works?'

'I shan't be interfering with your plans. You go ahead. But I need somewhere for tonight. Only tonight. By tomorrow it will all be over.' The fair-haired man pulled a face.

'Ivan, it's very risky...'

'Mirko, just think about it. It doesn't affect you; I'm the only one in danger.' The fair-haired man wiped the sweat off his forehead.

'All right. Come round whenever you want,' said Mirko wearily. He switched off his mobile and put it back in his pocket, placed his elbows on the paper and tried to continue reading. But he kept losing the thread and missing lines. So, Ivan was back! Now it could only end in a bloodbath. He leafed through the paper from beginning to end without taking in a word.


The man with the red moustache knocked on the door and went into the study. The vicar was waiting for him, seated at his desk. He did not get up. but waited for the visitor to cross the whole length of the room in silence.

'I don't like the news I'm getting, Kowalski!' he said sharply, putting two little bottles of spray back into a drawer.

'We're working on it, Your Eminence. Salazar has vanished from the hospital, we don't know how. The only people who can have helped him are the angels of death. That's the proof that he was in cahoots with them all along,' the man said defensively.

'I couldn't care less about any of that! And anyway, I don't think it's quite so clear-cut, Kowalski. Salazar is no fool. He is a hound of God. They've trained him well. Did you think you could cow him with a death threat? Within just a few days that fiend has managed to flush out a euthanasiast; you were on the job for months without managing anything at all. Now you have caused him to slip through our fingers with your persecution mania; and I don't think that your men in Holland are doing much better!' The vicar got up suddenly and went towards the window; looking out at the changing pattern of the flowers in the garden below sometimes had a soothing effect.

'Have you at least downloaded the files from that scientist's computer?' he asked with unaccustomed courtesy.

'The hard disks had already been removed by someone, probably by Pertiwi himself. We don't know where they're hidden. So we burned the lot, just to be on the safe side.'

'So even that Darwinist's archives are beyond our reach!' remarked the vicar with an effort at self-control, still contemplating the subtly-coloured flower-bed.

'We're going through Salazar's flat in Amsterdam. We think he may have copies of his friend's research,' proffered Kowalski nervously.

'Yes, that friend who slipped through your fingers and who is still alive!' shot back the vicar, finally detaching his gaze from the flower-bed and turning it upon the man with the red moustache. He went back to his desk and sat down, drumming his fingers nervously on the table.

'We set this whole thing up so as to lure Salazar to Rome, and you let him give us the slip. We should have intercepted him, dismantled his network of syncretists and got our hands on Pertiwi's research. Now the whole thing's gone up in smoke!' observed the vicar, continuing his effort at self-control.

'Your Eminence, all is not yet lost. We are on Pertiwi's trail; our agents are on his heels. And Salazar won't make it out of Rome. He's done for; he thinks he can outsmart us…' Kowalski's attempt at a damage limitation exercise seemed to leave the prelate unconvinced. He opened a drawer in the desk and took out Salazar's china pipe-cum-holy-water sprinkler.

'Kowalski, do you know what this is?' he asked him, dangling the thing in front of the red moustache. Kowalski took the pipe and turned it over in his hands.

'A holy-water sprinkler!' he said, narrowing his eyes.

'Exactly…' replied the vicar, stretching out a hand to regain possession of the object. He dropped it back into the drawer and said, almost to himself:

'This is too much – he must be killed.'

'And so he shall, Your Eminence!'

'You may go now, Kowalski! And don't come back until you've got results,' the vicar snapped without even bothering to raise his head; eye contact was not for him.


It was late afternoon when Pablo had arrived outside the storeroom. As he passed the door, he glanced inside. Some workmen were stowing things on to the lorry parked in the courtyard. The red-faced one nearest the doorway, his overall unbuttoned to the waist, was drinking water from a bottle; he glanced at Pablo absent-mindedly as he wiped his mouth. Inside, a radio was blaring. Glancing sunlight fell through the skylights, causing the men's shadows to flicker over the end wall. The first-floor offices were empty, the blinds lowered. On the ground floor, next to the storeroom, was a changing-room with small cupboards and two benches up against the wall. Pablo walked round the building until he came to the courtyard. Wooden duck-boarding and cans of paraffin cluttered the narrow space, which was entered through a gate of stakes and rusty bedsprings, with a chain and padlock hanging from it; but it was open. Weeds were sprouting from the walls and pavement; the place was largely in shadow, but the pile of cans was in partial sunlight. Two workmen were standing on the truck and the others were passing crates up to them. Inside the storeroom, the red-faced man was now singing along to the music on the radio at the top of his voice; another man was begging him to stop. The narrow alleyway led to the back of other hangars. There were few shops in the neighbourhood, just a tobacconist on one corner of the avenue. A few desolate blocks of flats were perched at the crest of a rise, surrounded by tangled undergrowth. Dreary edge-of-town streets; rubbish-strewn ditches; illegal immigrants' shacks among scrubby bushes. Pablo retraced his steps to the avenue and went to wait for the others under the bus shelter. It was four against four; they couldn't afford to make any mistakes. They pushed the car up against the gate at the back. The truck was now fully loaded, the ropes firmly secured; the radio had been switched off. The workmen were in the changing-room, their voices audible above the noise of the shower. Pablo put on the belt with his toolkit, opened the gate and jumped up on to the truck. This was the trickiest bit: he had only a moment to locate the correct crate. He found it under several others, two smaller crates of oil-lamps and some cans of fuel oil. The others were standing by with the replacement boxes of candles. They passed them up to him hurriedly, almost holding their breath while Mirko, in the driving seat, had his hand on the ignition key. If something went wrong now, that would be that. Pablo didn't have time to secure one end of the rope; the workmen's voices were getting louder, they were coming out of the changing-room. He slipped through the gate and ran off with the others; Mirko reversed slowly after them. At the end of the alleyway they all climbed in, closing the doors quietly behind them. They stopped on a track in the countryside around Torre Lupata and threw the candles into a canal.

That night Marta woke up suddenly, drenched with sweat. She had had a nightmare, but she couldn't remember any details, only a vague sense of dread, and a series of rambling images. She checked the time: four in the morning. Her eyes were still burning with tiredness, but she could not get back to sleep. She tossed and turned; every fold in the sheet felt like a blade. Finally she got up and went to get a drink of water from the kitchen. Or milk, perhaps: she'd read somewhere that milk had a calming effect; she took a gulp straight out of the carton, but it was too cold. She went back into the bedroom and curled up on a chair, pulling a blanket round her shoulders and glancing out at the street through the shutters: one winking traffic light and four large rubbish bins. Everything was laid out ready on a chair: her clothes, the train tickets, her suitcase, a guide to Venice. She had to look like a tourist. By now the substitute candles would be in place, but she wouldn't know how it had gone until the next day. All contacts put on hold until Thursday, by which time they would all be well out of Rome. What about Ivan? There was no way out for him. Mirko had told her that he'd come to Rome to kill Novak, but Ivan himself hadn't said a word about it. Why not? Did he not trust her? Or, yet again, was it so that she wouldn't get any fancy ideas? Trying to kill Novak was tantamount to suicide. Even if he did manage to fire a shot, he was doomed anyway. Marta sensed that it was late. She saw herself, on the run once again, in yet another house, another town. More safe houses, more shadowing, more attacks, cocaine capsules hidden amongst the Omega

Three, the dealers' suspicious faces, weapons slipped into her handbag, the panic that seized her at the sight of a man in uniform. And that enduring sense of loneliness, that fear. The impossibility of even sitting down quietly on a park bench. How would it all end? Sooner or later, they'd get her. Suppose she fell ill? Worse still, she might end up in prison. But might she not also come through unscathed? If only she had managed to persuade Ivan to stay with her. They could have got out of there, they could have gone away together, perhaps even to America. It was still possible.

She remembered a distant September afternoon they'd spent together by the sea; the sand had looked positively black in the setting sun, the bathing attendants were folding up the deckchairs and the hawkers were wheeling carts piled high with unsold clothes up the concrete walkways all along the beach, their long shadows weaving over the white walls of the bathing-huts. An old fisherman up to his waist in water was scrabbling doggedly about in the sand in search of clams; he had the hard, rough skin of a man who has spent the whole summer in the sun. She and Ivan had sat down at the water's edge.

'Look! If you go far enough out, you'll come to America...' Ivan had said meaningfully, looking towards the setting sun.

'Rubbish: if you go far enough out, you'll come to Sardinia,' she had replied, taking the wind out of his sails. They'd both burst out laughing, hugging one another and rolling round in the sand, two bodies forming one joyful whole. Those were the days when anything could make them laugh until they cried. Everything was still in place, everything was possible. The sound of a bus driving off from the traffic lights interrupted Marta's train of thought. Outside, it was getting light; the room was slowly emerging from the darkness. Marta picked her clothes up from the chair and dressed herself; she was in no hurry. She put on her make-up carefully while the coffee gurgled on the stove. When she went out into the street, the first rays of sun were coming in through the blinds and falling on to the suitcase she had left in the bedroom.

After a supper of lentil soup at a table with a group of beggars, he had slept in a refuge run by Caritas. At first light he had got up from the camp-bed and gone out. Empty buses were arriving in the station forecourt. The bells of the first Easter Day mass could just be heard above the clanging of the overhead railway. On the wall of the ticket-office in the bus station Salazar found a map of the bus routes between there and the sea. He studied the coastline, trying to work out where he might have been held captive. A thick pinewood, low-rise holiday homes, abut half an hour out of town. He located two possibilities: the stretch of coast between Fregene and Focene, or the coast around Castel Fusano. Going towards Ostia it was all too built up. The sudden sharp curves ruled out Castel Fusano; to get to Rome from there it would make more sense to take Via Cristoforo Colombo, which was completely straight. The planes that he had heard suggested Fregene or Focene, which were not far from Fiumicino Airport. Salazar rested his finger on the map and began working out how to board the next bus to Fregene. He had to act fast. He could try begging, but there was hardly anyone around, and it would be slow work. Robbing someone outright would be dangerous. So he went into a self-service restaurant in the station and grabbed a fork from the cutlery section, then continued on to the Chapel of Saint Christopher, to the left of the station. Here his goal was the alms-box beneath the row of candles, one of which he lit, pretending to pray while rummaging around in the lock with his fork; at last it broke, yielding up a pile of coins he slipped quickly into his track-suit pocket. He acknowledged the patron saint of travellers with a sign of the cross and left the chapel almost at a run.

He got out at the first stop in Fregene, in front of the police barracks, and went into a bar on the other side of the road. Now he had to find the baker's shop. He ordered a coffee and drank it at the counter, taking his time. Choosing his moment, when the place was empty, he went up to the barman and asked:

'Excuse me, can you tell me where the bakeries are here in Fregene? I'm a baker and I'm looking for temporary work.'

The barman was drying the glasses.

'A bakery?' he said, turning towards the cashier for further details. It was she who answered for him:

'There's Albanesi's here on the square, or else De Piscopo, near the church. Otherwise you'll have to go to Fiumicino.'

'Which way is the church?'

'Here in the pinewood. What's the name of the street?' she asked, turning to her colleague for assistance. But Salazar had already left the bar.

Some trails of mist still lingered in the pinewood. He found the church by following the people who were going to mass, then wandered the nearby streets until he caught the smell of freshly-baked bread. De Piscopo's bakery was a low building with metal-framed doors and windows and an ugly garish green shop sign. Salazar walked past it and took a road between the trees which gradually narrowed; parts of the asphalt were covered in sand. The villas were thinning out, their entrance gates becoming higher. It was not long before he recognized the view he had seen from the window of the basement; the house in which he had been held stood in a curve of the road. Although the surrounding villas were luxurious in the extreme, this one had no garden and the area around it was choked with weeds; the blinds were down, the windowsills were covered with moss and the eaves had tufts of grass growing in them. A rusty flagpole hung above the peeling door. Perhaps it had once been a Forestry Commission Station, which had been turned into a holiday home and then abandoned. Salazar walked round the building and found a back window he thought he could force open. He found a piece of wood in the undergrowth and managed to raise the blind, then broke the window, turned the handle and climbed in. Everything inside seemed to be in order: a house shut up for the holidays, with mattresses rolled up on their springs and wardrobes open to let in the air. He found the living room with the long table and the dusty pottery; he also found the basement where he had been held. He inspected each room carefully, but the members of the Free Death Brigade had left no sign of their earlier presence. He paid a cursory visit to the kitchen, and was about to leave when he noticed a lump of something white stuck to the stove; at first he thought it was mould, but when he touched it, it felt like plastic, or hardened glue. As he walked around, he noticed that the floor was sticky, and the sink was encrusted with that same resin-like material. He opened the cupboards, inspected plates and glasses, pulled out all the saucepans; the larger ones were still damp, their interiors coated with something white. He looked in the dustbin and found a piece of candle. So, someone had been melting wax. He searched the place for other clues. Bathroom, bedrooms and living room revealed nothing. He went out to the back of the house and poked around in the undergrowth, where he found a series of large white plastic tubes which had been cut lengthways; they were three inches wide and about a metre and a half in length. Inside, his fingers came upon lumps of wax similar to those he had found in the kitchen. Now he was beginning to see the light and, as he did so, he felt a sudden shudder of horror creep down his spine. Clearly, the members of the Free Death Brigade had been making candles, and big ones at that. Not to light in front of altars, but more probably to serve as explosive devices. They were to replace the ones on the papal podium in Saint Peter's Square and send everything sky-high! Now Salazar saw why the man who had questioned him had been so interested in the police patrols on the podium! He clenched his fists and cursed himself. Yet in fact he had nothing to reproach himself for. It was only by answering those questions that he had had any chance of getting out of their clutches. Anyway, there might still be time. He looked down at himself, covered in scratches from the brambles, dressed like a beggar, his pockets weighed down with small change. It was not an encouraging sight.

The De Piscopo bread van was parked outside the bakery with the engine running and the door open. Between blaring adverts, the radio was giving out the traffic news. The driver had gone into the shop to take the orders and was chatting with the baker; two shop boys were lazily piling the bread into the baskets, cackling as they did so and occasionally gesturing towards the window. They loaded up a couple of trays of pastries and went into the back of the shop. Salazar observed the scene from behind a rubbish bin. He walked around the bread van, jumped into the driving seat and drove off, skidding over the gravel. The driver came out of the shop, put his hands on his hips, shook his head with a smile and went back into the shop, thinking the shop boys were playing a joke on him.

Salazar turned into the road which led to the Aurelia, the curves reminding him of the route he had been taken on, blindfolded, by the members of the Free Death Brigade. He had to act fast; the ceremony would be starting in an hour. It was a glorious day; the air was crystal-clear, fields and houses crisply outlined, barely blurred by the thinning mist on the windscreen. The rows of cluster pines were giving off a fresh scent of resin, casting sharp shadows on the tender green of the fields. The roads around the city were strangely empty, but by the time he got to Via Cipro the pilgrims' buses were already double-parked, and columns of visitors snaked like gigantic caterpillars from one pavement to the other. Salazar abandoned De Piscopo's van and carried on on foot. People were pouring into the square; but before going to the colonnade, they had to be searched. Policemen were going through bags and running metal detectors over their owners. A large stand had been put up on the side overlooking Via della Conciliazione, with numbered paying places, and special areas for official visitors. The crowd was buzzing with impatience; children were climbing on to their parents' shoulders and craning their necks in the direction of the basilica. Many people had brought along plastic stools and were standing on them to get a better view. Although it was barely ten o'clock, the sun was already hot. Water sellers with red caps were weaving their way along the screened-off corridors, while policemen directed people towards the less crowded parts of the square. Salazar had decided to make a discreet approach to a Swiss Guard and give the alarm, so as to avoid creating sudden panic. The Swiss Guards were the only ones he trusted. But the nearest ones were just in front of the papal podium. He was trying to worm his way through the throng to reach them when he heard someone calling him.

'Well, if it isn't Salazar! So you're here too! Well, of course you are! We wouldn't miss this for anything!'

The guarantor of faith was coming towards him, all dressed in white, wiping the sweat from his forehead with a handkerchief.

'That's an odd get-up you're wearing! Were you thinking of running the marathon? Actually, sporting gear isn't a bad wheeze. I'm already boiling in this gabardine,' he added, loosening his tie. His eyes on the basilica, Salazar sought desperately for an excuse to get away. But the doctor rambled on, nodding and winking in the direction of the podium.

'You'll see, we've done a grand job,' he said in a low voice.

'Papal medicine is in the vanguard when it comes to the preservation of corpses,' he continued. 'Of course modern refrigeration techniques are crucial here. My predecessors completely dehydrated Ratzinger's body after his death; we did the rest. We kept nature well away from that coffin. Basically, inspector, that is the essence of every miracle: the suspension of the laws of nature. As you see, we're getting there! You might say that the Kingdom of Heaven will come when man has succeeded in suspending the laws of nature altogether. It's all much simpler than you think!' Squinting against the sun, the doctor continued dabbing his forehead with his handkerchief. He raised his sweat-drenched eyebrows and carried on talking, despite the effort that it seemed to cost him, even giving a faintly gleeful smile.

'Do you know, inspector, I was thinking of you as I was getting ready to come out this morning. I was also thinking about angels: I was thinking that all the angelic orders are probably here at this very moment. If the pope's body is found to be intact, it will be a portentous event, a miracle such as has not occurred for centuries. The angelic orders could not miss

out on such an occasion, so here they'll all be, from the Powers
to the Dominions and the Principalities. The archangels will
be here too, probably the odd Seraph. I don't know about the
Thrones, they're rather busy, particularly at Easter; I'm not sure
about the Cherubim, either, that would be too dangerous. As
you know, Cherubim are referred to as the 'burning ones'; the
heat produced by such a high concentration of burning angels
would be unbearable for us humans, we'd all end up fried! The
ones who'll be here in force are the Virtues, the angels who
inspire men to excel in art and science. So why not try to make
contact with them? It shouldn't be difficult. All you need is to
locate the lightning flashes they produce. We are in no doubt
about the ways that angels reveal themselves. The Bible is quite
clear in this respect: the Powers are surrounded by coloured
auras and misty vapours, the Principalities by rays of light and
the Virtues by lightning. Do you know what I think, Salazar? I
think that not enough is made of these possibilities of contact
between humanity and the celestial sphere. We must not let
this chance slip through our fingers; such opportunities occur
just a few times in a millennium, it will be centuries before
another such occurs. One mustn't overdo it with miracles; they
tend to lose their lure. But we are men of science and have
little to do with such mass events; we should have prepared
ourselves for this one by establishing contact with the angelic
world in order to organize a human-angelic meeting in tandem
with the ceremony. Times have changed, mankind is no longer
sunk in barbarism; we are now sufficiently mature to engage
in dialogue with these first offshoots of divinity. Think of the
good that could come of it! The Eternal Father Himself would
benefit; people would have greater faith in the coming of the
Kingdom of Heaven. How could the curia not have thought of
that? What about the angelic hierarchies themselves? Has it

not occurred to anyone that here on earth, after more than two thousand years, we are beginning to need some pretty powerful signs? The Archangel Michael should have given the matter some thought...' The doctor shook his head; a drop of sweat had fallen on to his lip, and then on to the white hairs of his goatee beard. Salazar looked at him with something verging on distaste, then turned his gaze towards the crowd in front of him, seeking a way through.

'Excuse me, I really don't have time...' he said, then pushed his way into the throng.

'Whoa there, inspector, you're always in such a rush! Now, shall I tell you what I think? In my view, angels themselves aren't big on communication, one department doesn't know what the other is doing! Besides, if you were one of the Cherubim, would you be bothered with an angel from the third sphere? You mark my words, they're just like us in the curia, all busy feathering their own nests! I tell you, it's "I'm all right Jack" up there too. And if they can't be bothered, why should we? Where are you dashing off to now, inspector? Come with me, I've got a place on the podium, we'll be more comfortable there. I've even brought my binoculars!' he shouted, waving a black case he wore around his neck. But Salazar was out of earshot; now he was struggling forward through the crowd, shoving, apologizing, squeezing himself into the slightest gap in his effort to reach the barrier.

Ivan was hurrying down Borgo Santo Spirito, picking his way amidst a swarm of children. He was already in the square, all he had to do now was follow the crowd. Seeing an opening, he broke out of the queue and came up against the guards with their metal detectors. He had to find a way of concealing his pistol from them; he felt for it in his jacket, then looked around. A group of pilgrims were clustering around their leader's brightly-coloured umbrella; a group of nuns was lining up for the safety check. Seated pedlars were selling drinks and souvenirs; one had a variety of toy animals on a string, Mickey Mouse, Pluto and Minnie. Salazar selected a Minnie; for good measure, he also purchased a tee-shirt with a portrait of Benedict XVI and the words 'Canonize him pronto' beneath it. He went into a doorway and slipped it on, then tore open the cloth on Minnie's back and slipped his Glock down into the foam rubber. He scrutinized the crowd around him and settled on a father with a small girl on his shoulders.

'I found this on the ground. Is it yours?' The man shook his head, but the child held out her hand.

'Would you like it?' Ivan asked, smiling invitingly. The little girl nodded, burying her face in her father's shoulder. Again, the man shook his head.

'Well then, I'll just have to throw it away!' said Ivan with mock regret. The father gave the child a kindly grin of surrender, then finally nodded himself. Ivan tenderly handed her the toy, then took his place in the queue behind the man. The guard smiled at the child, drawing the metal detector down her back as he did so, then pinched her cheek and said '*Ciao*' to her as he walked away. Once in the square, Ivan followed the pair, keeping an eye on the child's red dress. When he saw the man stop on the left-hand side of the colonnade, he approached him cautiously, until he was right behind him. At that moment a sudden cry went up in the square. The pope had gone on to the podium and was taking his place on the throne. All eyes were on the big screens, and thunderous applause broke out. Ivan took advantage of it to grab the toy and drop it on the ground. Bending down to pick it up, he thrust his hand into the foam rubber, extracted the pistol and put it in his belt.

'You dropped her again!' he said, proffering Minnie to the child, who hugged the creature to her with a look of outrage. The father turned to thank him, his expression conveying apologies for his child's excesses. Ivan walked off, elbowing his way firmly through the crowd, which parted at his approach, clearly offended by his rough and ready manner.

Crushed against the barrier, Marta peered constantly over her shoulder. She had been one of the first to take her place, shortly after daybreak. Tired, thirsty, her face burned by the sun, she was still hoping to intercept Ivan and dissuade him from that act of madness. She inspected the podium: Novak was there, wearing his cardinal's mozetta and damask mitre. In front of him, the servers had just lit the wicks of the four great candles on the altar. Now they were coming down from the podium in an orderly file and taking their places to either side of it. Marta was quite aware that staying put was tantamount to allowing herself to become trapped, but it was the only way to meet up with Ivan. This was the best place from which to fire. The crowd was separated from the podium by a cordon of Swiss Guards. Two prelates in cardinals' robes had taken their places beside the pope. On the façade of the basilica, the cloth covering the giant portrait of Joseph Ratzinger, smiling benignly on the crowd, had now been lifted. The ceremony was beginning. The procession bearing the coffin of Benedict XVI arrived at the foot of the podium. Four altar-boys hoisted it on to their shoulders and laid it at the foot of the altar. The deacon opened the Evangeliary on the lectern and stood back to receive the censer. Clouds of incense swirled around the coffin, and a choir of white-clad choristers intoned a chant. When they fell silent, the pope rose to his feet and raised his arms. The crowd too fell suddenly silent. By now the sun was high in the Roman sky.

At last Salazar had reached the barrier in front of the right side of the podium. He started to wave his hands, hoping to attract the attention of the Swiss Guards, but they seemed impervious to his efforts, unwilling to pay him any attention. He was not helped by the fact that a thousand other people were gesticulating in the direction of the television cameras on their revolving stands and waving their white and yellow flags. Salazar tied himself into knots in his efforts to make himself seen, but to no avail. Then he had the idea of throwing empty plastic bottles at the podium, and that seemed to be more effective. The Swiss Guards gave each other worried looks and appeared to be on the point of taking action. But then an eager-beaver of a plainclothes-policeman crept up behind him, seized him by the collar of his tracksuit and dragged him backwards, trying to wrestle him to the ground. Salazar shook him off but made no effort to run away, indeed he stood there making deferential gestures. The plainclothes-policeman did not seem reassured, but seized him by the shoulders and started to drag him off towards the guard post. Not wishing to arouse attention, Salazar allowed himself to be manhandled, attempted to reason with the man, apologized, tried to explain that he absolutely had to talk to one of the Swiss Guards. But the plainclothes-man didn't want to hear any explanations from such a grubby, unshaven, swarthy and evil-smelling individual; indeed, he gestured to his colleagues to come and give him a hand. At this point Salazar lost his temper. He kneed the man in the stomach, causing him to fall forwards, then hit him in the face. All around, people were now shouting in alarm; a small space opened up in the crowd, dense though it was, and for a short time the two men slugged it out. Then the plainclothes-man fell to the ground and Salazar once more slipped off into the throng. Behind him, other plainclothes-men were jumping up into the air in their efforts to keep track of him.

Now they were converging, though they couldn't see each other. Marta Quinz, Ivan Zago and Salazar were all pushing their way forwards towards the same point in the square; Ivan had his hand on the pistol in his pocket, scanning the podium for his quarry. He would have to take aim fast and fire instantly; if anyone saw him taking the weapon out of his pocket, the slightest nudge would cause him to miss his target. Ideally, he should be up at the barrier, but he was afraid that would take too long. The shots would spread panic, and Novak might get away. Marta was peering around her desperately, trying to locate him, looking anxiously at her watch. There were only a few minutes to go. Salazar was making his way purposefully forward, determined to jump the barrier; he knew the marksmen would fire, but he might just have time to save himself by throwing himself at the feet of the Swiss Guards, thus ensuring himself a possibility of protection.

The pope had stood up on the podium and was walking towards the coffin; four servers stood at the four sides, ready to lift the lid. The telecameras were now all trained on the august inlaid table; the crowd were holding their breath, eyes glued to the big screens. A child let out a wail. Pigeons cooed in the eerie silence. Then the pope raised his arms, and a roar went through the square. The prelates on the podium fell to their knees, the choir launched into an Alleluia and images of Benedict XVI's body, intact on the faded velvet quilt, were beamed throughout the world. There on the big screens the sallow face, thin lips and goggle eyes caused children to wail and adults to exult. A wave of emotion swept through the square. People hugged one another, someone fainted and was promptly attended to, borne aloft like a hero; nuns with their eyes raised skywards prayed silently, clutching their crucifixes; banners fluttered, thousands of clapping hands sent a burst of applause rippling through the square. Ivan lifted his pistol, took aim between the heads of two friars, and fired. Marta had turned round just in time to see him, right behind her, before she was swallowed again up by the roaring crowd. A few metres away, Salazar had climbed over the barrier and was zigzagging towards the podium. Four Swiss Guards threw themselves on him amidst the marksmen's shots.

At that same moment, on the embankment of the Lungotevere, Mirko took his mobile out of his pocket and looked up towards the gleaming dome of Saint Peter's towering above the line of other buildings. His hands were trembling as he pressed the re-dial key. The screen lit up, and a few seconds later a thunderous roar tore through the air.

Anyone observing the shrieking, jostling crowd from the basilica would have seen snarling faces crushed up against barriers, bodies slowly suffocated by the sheer weight of the mass behind them; some of the more ruthless were fighting their way out of the sea of heads and shoulders and throwing themselves over the barriers, over the trampled bodies of the dead, their hands outstretched in search of some handhold that would enable them to extricate themselves from that tangle of bodies. Black smoke was rising from the burning podium, bits of charred paper floating through the air. The pope's body, wrapped in a purple cloak, was being dragged up the flight of steps by the Swiss Guards. Prelates were propping one other up, gesturing to the first stretcher-bearers who were now running down the steps of the sacristy. Survivors were staggering amongst upturned chairs, shoes, mitres and blood-stained tunics. Benedict XVI's bier had shattered and the body had rolled on to the paving, where it now lay: contorted, his arms strangely raised, his chasuble riding up above his tunic, Joseph Ratzinger looked like a manikin dressed as a bride. Salazar got up from his kneeling position and peered through the smoke. Immediately after the explosion, the guards had let go of him and rushed towards the podium, leaving him in the hands of a stunned-looking soldier. Salazar had then fainted; as he came to, he ran his hands cautiously over his body; his head was spinning, his vision blurred, but no serious damage seemed to have been done. Scrabbling on the ground as he tried to get to his feet, he came upon something hard; looking at it more closely, he saw a glass eye with a blue iris.

# Epilogue

It was a sombre moon that rose above the rooftops of Rome
that night. Helicopters were no longer flying over the city, but
sirens were still blaring in the streets. Guards were posted on
bridges and outside government offices and churches. Police
at road-blocks pointed their submachine guns at every car that
passed. In their homes, people were glued to their televisions
where a series of grave faces were engaging in speeches of
condolence in front of images of apparently endless scenes
of massacre. Salazar sat down on a bench under the palm
trees in Piazza del Risorgimento. He was tired and hungry,
aching in every limb. The din of the explosion, the shouts, the
bloodied faces had brought back buried memories of the day
when Port-au-Prince had toppled in the quake. He smelt the
same stench of scorched flesh, sweat and excrement. He felt
again that ancient fear, which came not from within, but had
been unleashed upon him by the boundless sky. He felt at last
that he was free, that now he could go anywhere he wanted.
No one was now his master, no one would look for him. A
new life opened up before him, as on the day he had emerged,
weeping, from the rubble of his home. The papal policeman
Domingo Salazar was no more. He was dead, he'd vanished,
along with old Bonardi, his own friend Guntur, the vicar with

the glass eye and indeed Pope Benedict XVIII himself. But he didn't know what to do with all that freedom. He had no home to go to, no kith or kin, no ties. He had been reared and trained to defend the Holy Mother Church and that was all he knew how to do. Away from his army, far from his battlefield, his life would make no sense. He was a *domini canis*, a hound of God, God's dog, and all he could do was serve his master. And what is a dog without a master? Salazar looked up at the dome of Saint Peter's in the moonlight, stood up unsteadily and limped towards the gate of the Porta Angelica. He stood to attention and gave the military salute to the Swiss Guard in the sentry box beyond the gate.

'I am the missing agent Domingo Salazar, registration number 18246592NLA, and I've come to give myself up for an identity check.' Pointing his halberd at his back, the soldier escorted his quarry into the building.

# Praise for Diego Marani

## New Finnish Grammar

*New Finnish Grammar* won 3 literary prizes in Italy: the Premio Grinzane Cavour, Premio Ostia Mare and Premio Giuseppe Desi. The Dedalus translation by Judith Landry won The Oxford Weidenfeld Translation Prize and was shortlisted for the Independent Foreign Fiction Award, The Best Translated Book Award and the Europe Book Prize.

"It is about loss of language, disorientation and survival in a state of translation. Its hero is constructed only by language – he's a kind of replicant. The novel is melancholy, wide-ranging and sensitive, and its many inventive strands placed Judith Landry in a similar position to the protagonist's in many ways, since the story required her to carry across Finnishness as well as Italian, and to convey the sense of profound estrangement that the novel inhabits. The plotting sets one story inside another, including retellings of the *Kalevala* and dream journeys of the Nordic shamans. It is a highly original, uniquely imagined work. In the words of one of the judges, 'it's a meditation on the whole phenomenon of language-learning and foreignness'."

Marina Warner at The Oxford-Weidenfeld Translation Prize
Award Ceremony

"It was, naturally, the flatness of the title that attracted me: it bespoke, in its quiet confidence, a deep, rich and eventful inner life. And besides, I have some inkling of what Finnish grammar is like: fiendishly complex, basically, and related to no other languages on earth save Hungarian and Estonian (I simplify). Learning Finnish involves not only beginning to appreciate the most beautiful of languages, but grasping, among many, many other things, 15 cases for nouns, such as the inessive, the elative, the ilative, and, everyone's favourite, the abessive. I will return to the abessive in a minute. Deep and rich, did I say? That isn't the half of it. I can't remember when I read a more extraordinary novel, or when I was last so strongly tempted to use the word 'genius' of its author."

Nick Lezard's Choice in *The Guardian*

"A wounded sailor is found on a Trieste quay – amnesiac, unable to speak and with nothing to identify him except a name tag pointing to Finnish origins. A passing doctor resolves to teach him Finnish to restore his memory and rebuild his identity. Charming and beguiling."

Books of the Year in *The Financial Times*

"...an entrancing, disturbing exploration of the limits of speech and self."                    Boyd Tonkin in *The Independent*

"Beautifully written and translated, and beautifully original."

Kate Saunders in *The Times*

"Marani has created a staggering study of loss and an act of retrieval that is heroic... Marani's moving novel about the brutal displacement imposed by war and fate achieves consummate emotional intelligence. The sailor is left wondering how on earth he ended up in Trieste in the first place. He never unravels the truth; the doctor does and that is his share of a very human tragedy."                    Eileen Battersby in *The Irish Times*

"The title is odd, the cover is grey and the author is a besuited Eurocrat. But beneath these unflamboyant exteriors lie a colourful story. It has taken 10 years, the dedication of a small UK publisher and a perfect-pitch translation to deliver Diego Marani's first novel in English. When it came out in Italian, reviewers called it a masterpiece and it won several prizes. Since then Marani has written five more novels and become a Euro-celebrity."                    Rosie Goldsmith in *The Independent*

"Judith Landry is to be congratulated on her seamless translation from the Italian, and Dedalus for introducing English readers to a fascinating writer."
                    Gabriel Josipovici in *The New Statesman*

"One somehow knows that this couldn't have been written by an English writer. It has a thoroughly European sensibility: intellectual, melancholy, mysterious, imbued with a sense of tragedy and history."
                    Brandon Robshaw in *The Independent on Sunday*

"...a thoughtful, idiosyncratic book and, in its utter disdain for the conventions of literary realism, entirely to be applauded."
                    Joanna Kavenna in *The Literary Review*

"There is an unyieldingness at the heart of Diego Marani's novel. He presents a world where heroism is expended in a futile task, friendship is sacrificed to despair, and help is rendered in such a way as to further the disaster. Yet this book is full of riches: a landscape so solidly created one can hear the ice crack, a moving examination of what makes a human being, and a restless brooding over the ideas of memory, belonging and identity (all three main characters are in some way lost). It is written in mirror-smooth prose and superbly translated. The story, finally, can't fail."

Anita Mason in *The Warwick Review*

"Don't be put off by the unwelcoming title: this is an extraordinary book, as good as Michael Ondaatje's *The English Patient* and with a similar mystery at its heart."

Cressida Connolly in *The Spectator's Books of the Year*

"...we soon forget we are reading an English translation of an Italian novel. Sheer narrative vim is one reason for this... What gives *New Finnish Grammar* its true interest, however, is its evocation of a place and language foreign to the author yet, to all appearances, intimately familiar."

Oliver Ready in *The Times Literary Supplement*

"As well as raising questions concerning psyche, identity and nationality, Sampo's confused agony is quite simply one of the most incisive reflections of the trauma that befell Europe during that period that one might ever read."

Oliver Basciano in *ArtReview*

"I know that it is a book that I will be thrusting into peoples hands for years to come urging them to buy it, read it and spread the word. It is the least that I can do for the pleasure that it has given me."

Broad Conversation from Blackwell's Bookshop in Oxford

# The Last of the Vostyachs

*The Last of the Vostyachs* won 2 literary prizes in Italy: the Premio Campiello and Premio Stresa. The Dedalus translation by Judith Landry was longlisted for The Independent Foreign Fiction Award.

"A 'genius' Helsinki mystery with a touch of The Killing... So, we have: 1. An intellectual puzzle. 2. A wild man of nature adrift in a big city. 3. A policier set near the Arctic Circle. (If that alone doesn't make you put down your copies of Fifty Shades of Whatever then I despair. It has that Killingesque atmosphere.) 4. Magic, and a sense of the immensity of the primeval universe. 5. An unmistakable dash of humour, even when your nerves are being shredded. 6. Wolves, and a Siberian tiger, let loose from a zoo. 7. A happy ending against all odds. And 8. All hanging together. When I reviewed *New Finnish Grammar*, I edged towards using the word 'genius' to describe Marani. I'm doing so again now."

Nick Lezard's Choice in *The Guardian*

"For Italian fiction in translation, there is nobody more important being published today. This is a beautiful, intelligently funny novel." *Italia Magazine*

"Marani twists a great, atmospheric – alternately frigid and very heated – story around this in this intellectual, linguistic, and just good old-fashioned-type thriller, culminating in Aurtova going down in flames as he closes what was to be his grand speech-of-a-lifetime with an impassioned, deluded: 'Long live Finland! Long live ignornace!' This – and many other scenes – can make you wish for a movie version, but in written form they do nicely too. There's linguistic theory (and terminology) woven in throughout the story, but that's just one layer of this nicely structured novel, which works well at all its different levels. Great fun, and highly recommended."

M.A. Orthofer in *The Complete Review*

"*The Last of the Vostyachs*, Diego Marani's second novel to appear in English, in a dazzling translation from the Italian by Judith Landry, is a riot of comic unpredictability... *The Last of the Vostyachs* cleverly explores notions of freedom, possession and imprisonment – erudition keeping pace with a rollicking plot. Marani's sentences are controlled explosions of impressionism, his narrative structure a thematic echo chamber." Max Liu in *The Times Literary Supplement*

"Landry is an adept translator, of the kind who likes to make it seem that the book has all along been written in English."

Matthew Reynolds in *The London Review of Books*

"In *The Last Of The Vostyachs*, the author's obsessions are still the same, language, it's purpose not merely as an instrument for communication, but also how it relates to the behavioural codes and cultural values that go to construct ones identity and that not only does language define the characteristics of a specific group or community, it is also the means by which an individual identifies themselves and how they identify with others. Although this time he has used them to create a fantastic clever, funny mystery/thriller complete with a wonderful villain, that you'll love to hate and whose exploits you'll be amazed and shocked by, all whilst laughing at him, especially in the end scenes... but I'll let you discover the delights of that moment."                                          *The Parish Lantern*

"Here , satire and farce rub shoulders with linguistic jargon, and comedy blends with grand guignol. Murder most foul stands beside the text of a speech to a congress of linguists. Marani slips effortlessly between styles. Particularly impressive is his command of the intricate details of phonetics. As a final gift to the reader, Marani is beautifully served by the sensitive translation from the original Italian."

Steve Walker in *Sunday Star Times of New Zealand*

"Part murder mystery set in the Arctic, part study of language, part Norse saga – though spliced with its own modernity, magic and humour – and part evocation of the Arctic wilderness. Marani's novel shows his extraordinary skills and erudition. He is well served by his translator, Judith Landry, who has produced a novel that appears to have been conceived in English."          Cathy Peake in *The Melbourne Saturday Age*

31901056274568